THE SEXY PART OF THE BIBLE

THE SEXY PART OF THE BIBLE

BY KOLA BOOF

This is a work of fiction. All names, characters, places, and incidents are the product of the author's imagination. Any resemblance to real events or persons, living or dead, is entirely coincidental.

Published by Akashic Books
©2011 Kola Boof

ISBN-13: 978-1-936070-96-1
Library of Congress Control Number: 2010939108

Akashic Books
PO Box 1456
New York, NY 10009
info@akashicbooks.com
www.akashicbooks.com

ACKNOWLEDGMENTS

If this book were to sell a million copies it still wouldn't be enough to express my gratitude to Johnny Temple, the publisher of Akashic Books.

My black American adoptive parents: I love you eternally. I see you, Father, watching over me. I love you forever.

I want to thank my new King, Posar A. Posr, for loving, accepting, and supporting me. I pray you'll always be my best friend.

I also want to thank my fans for not allowing my work to be silenced—I look forward to your feedback. The novel details the violent unfairness of identity; in a way, it's a compendium of my secrets; *the secret about hurting* . . . So I'm grateful for your love; I needed your love and there isn't a moment that I'm not thinking about your expectations and wanting to please you. Please know that I don't take this work lightly.

I have to thank the legendary New York University scholar, activist, and writer Derrick Bell for believing so strongly in this book. Ditto Nicholas Roman Lewis, who loved and nurtured the novel. I thank my sons Arnofo and Wombe for their indescribable telepathic support and understanding. One of my editors at Akashic, Ibrahim Ahmad, you've blessed my life and will be repaid. Chinweizu the Great: you are indeed my literary father. I thank the special women who inspired and held me up: Nafisa Goma, Ajowa Ifetayo, Aiesha Turman, Zakiya Padmore, Carol Mackey, Doreen Mununura, IsisPaperzZ (Twitter), my sister Erin McCargar in Tennessee, Beth Anne Zimmerman, and Rahel Thorsten. I'm very grateful, sisters. I thank Simon Palacio—for everything. Keidi Awadu, Rakesh Satyal, and Minister Brown—bless you for such giant small wishes!

for Nyibol Bior
Chuol apieth

The white woman is the virtuous part of the Bible;
her hand is fair.

—*The Christians of Ajowaland*
John Theodosius van Elker
1651

Orisha

You may as well know everything. That there are white men in Africa who no longer come to bring us the word of Jesus Christ, but come instead to bring back the dead. In fact, the man who brought *me* back to life, the only man I've ever trusted, the man who undid my virginity and now lies here dying, his head sweating profusely in my lap, is one of them. He is the tall Ron-Howard-as-Richie-Cunningham-from-*Happy-Days* one in our clinic whose given name from his white people is Stevedore. He is the one who makes me read books and teaches me how to better convince people that I am the character I'm playing. Surely I don't have to tell you how terribly young and liberal these foreign scientists are. How they bathe naked in the river with the Oluchi tribesmen, play American hip-hop music, and hang pictures of white dog-haired women in strips of cloth on their walls while they drip the DNA of dead people into flat, red-bottomed cups they call a "culture" . . . and cook food in this thing, the microwave. But what I do have to tell you about—and perhaps eventually the whole world—is how I have worshipped him so magnetically for all the nineteen years I've been alive again; and yet just this late afternoon, even as he is dying and my vision is blinded by sheets and sheets of tears, there is now nothing but the most silent betrayal and fascinating disbelief between us. It's because I know at last that the worst is true. The things we blacks have been whispering about in West Cassavaland since King Reagan was in the White House—that our dead are being cloned by foreign AIDS scientists. And as I hold Stevedore's last seconds of life, his head convulsing to the burnished heat of my bare black breasts, and try to keep his blue eyes from turning to glass, I know it now without a doubt that I, who never even had AIDS, am one of his clones. I feel like the monster in that book he forbade me to read as a child. But then again, this latest revelation allows me to finally call him Father. I also know now that it's my fault he never believed in God, and that this is why he named me the very last word to part his dying lips . . . *Eternity*.

Dear God and Dear Satan too: I address the both of you to say, "Ife kwulu ife akwudebe ya" (If one thing stands, another thing stands by it). For I am truly a descendent of the laboratory now, and I cry that You might take pity that he has made of me an actual goddess— as pathetic as either of You—an experimental daughter raised on weekends and during playtime by the Oluchi river women, yet privately educated and reared by what the Africans call the "Caucasoids." And just as when You created me—there's more poetry than sense to it.

It's my name that Stevedore calls right before his heart stops. He exhales it, passionately . . . *Eternity!* And though my tears prevent me from seeing the moment when his eyes become glass, I certainly feel it. Right now, especially, as hallucinatory memories come to me like some miracle story that the topless Oluchi women would expect tourists to believe, I can see *everything* that the American filmmakers have come here to make a motion picture about in my lover's glass-pane eyes.

I see the skeletal dog with the human arm in its

mouth, barely nourished enough to wag its tail as it runs away from the screaming mob. I see him, Stevedore, coming into the town square, only he's twenty years younger and resembles Richie Cunningham even more than he does now. Stevedore steps aside as the mutt he mistook for a Dalmatian runs past with my arm in its mouth. He's not surprised at all as he comes upon the sight of a frail, middle-aged Ajowan woman being kicked to death in the streets of DakCrete by the swallowers. To him, it is West Cassavaland desperation that causes the young people to kick me to death and stomp me and shout belligerently, "Kill the racist . . . kill the racist!" Stevedore is shocked, amazed, and horrified as their bony fists shake in the air, their black faces twisted with an urgent ejaculation as they, the swallowers, obliterate *me*—"The Racist." And he's lifting me now. Lifting me from my puddle of blood as my brains balloon out of my head like comic book clouds and my faint heart retires ever slowly, ever gently. My bowels release, splattering the front of his shirt, belt buckle, and zipper with warm, runny shit. And when he glances at the middle-aged Ajowan woman's face, bloody, wet, and asleep as though she's just been born, I can clearly see through his eyes that *she was me*. Me, exactly.

I can't think for a moment. I am the rum extract, the clone of this woman kicked to death in the streets. Only it's now again, the moment of your death, 2002, and I can't breathe without you, Stevedore. I glance up and there, shouting in the doorway, is Dr. Quicken, our scientist from Great Britain, his wrinkly pale throat rooster-red with excitement as he keeps insisting, "Eternity's killed him! . . . Eternity's killed the American!" People are coming—I hear them running toward the lab as Dr. Quicken cries out, "His shiny black bitch has killed him!"

As though peering into a puddle of elephant's piss, I can see myself in Dr. Quicken's cold, hateful, gray stare—my wicked flesh black as melted coal newly sprung from the earth's volcanic core. I can see my childlike saucer-shaped eyes and angular cheekbones fashioning my mouth into a blatant O, and my bare, skinny limbs bending toward the floor with your white-as-a-moon face in my lap. And for the first time, I know it's true what you used to say about me, Stevedore.

That I, Eternity, am *breathtaking*.

THE WOMEN'S DUNGEON, ABENI IBO PRISON

"I testified on your behalf," Stevedore's wife, Juliet, whispers to me.

She's carrying blankets and food, God bless her, because when you go to jail in West Cassavaland, they don't give you anything but a wire cot on a dirt floor with a hole in the middle to squat over. Worse than the fat green flies congregating around your shithole are the big brown rats quickly shooting from corner to corner with tails longer than teak braids, their toothy pointed noses sniffing to detect the smell of sand crystals on your toes or perspiration salt in the corners of your eyes and mouth. There are no bars or electricity down here. Just stone walls, torches, and stinking, unwashed women strewn about like skinny worm-infested dogs, and one of them is cuddling the only thing that I fear even more than rats—a doll. No matter how far away the woman is, the thing, the fucking doll, keeps staring at me! This is why I forget all about being mad at Juliet and break into tears and grab her and hug her, holding on for dear life when she arrives at my cell.

"I told the authorities everything," she exhales. Then, just as our embrace is beginning to feel comforting, she pulls away, saying, "As a formality, they're sending an investigator to the compound to ask some questions, but you're getting out of here tomorrow."

Tomorrow!?

Horrified of the coming hours and yet speechless, I gaze into Juliet Frankenheimer's frozen blue eyes as she seems to speak her sentences in categories: "I told them about you and my husband being in love—and how you worshipped him. I told them about Stevedore's hobby of writing plays and having you star in the sixteen-millimeter short comedies that he made to entertain the Oluchi and Ajowan people. I told them, Eternity, about how we found you abandoned on our doorstep and practically raised you from birth, and how Stevedore and I were just about to send you off to be educated in England. I told them about your high IQ and your gentle soul. I made them understand that there's no way in hell you'd ever harm a hair on Stevedore's body, you loved him so unselfishly. And being that I'm Stevedore's wife and have no reason to defend you, the Gon-ghossa Protectorate has decided to release you tomorrow."

It's all true, of course. I would have rather taken my own life than Stevedore's—but still, of all the scientists at the Africa Farms AIDS Clinic, why would Dr. Juliet be the one to come rushing to rescue me from the dungeon for criminals, witches, and people with AIDS? She has always hated my heart, the fact that it continues beating each day. She loathed Stevedore's penis to the point where she'd commissioned a nude portrait of him without one.

I watch her hand, its trembling fingers whiter than usual as she runs them through her limp blond hair. Then, suddenly, I realize that the redness in her eyes might not be from crying. She seems high to me. *Higher than a giraffe's pussy*, as Stevedore would say.

I blurt out two words: "Why, Juliet?"

"You think that just because you've hurt me so completely and for such a long time that I wouldn't still bring you justice? You should know me better than that, Eternity. You're my daughter, after all. No matter what went on between you and Stevedore, there's no way that I could ever harm either one of you. Hate comes from love. As your parents, we taught you all your life that when someone hates you, it's really because they love you so intensely. I couldn't leave you in this dump!"

"No, I meant to ask why perfectly intelligent, rational people would want to clone other humans."

"I should have never told you that you're a clone."

"But you weren't lying." My throat tightens and quivers as images from my screen test at the movie studio flicker in my mind like an evil slide show. And on the end of that, I call her "Mother."

"Listen," she whispers, pausing to think for a moment.

I am no longer listening; I am remembering. I can see myself in Dr. Juliet's sea-blue eyes. Only I am thirteen again, standing in the shade along the River Niger, my bloody hands held up to my face and my voice screaming for help as Stevedore rushes out of the foliage and into the riverbank, his bare white chest peeling in the middle, between the nipples, because he is one of those who burn in the sun, and he calms me and washes my girl-cave and waves my hands in the water and explains to me that it is only my monthly bleeding starting, and that this means I am officially a woman now and have the power, as we Ajowan women say, to bring back the dead.

And then I can see my bedroom in Juliet's blue eyes—Stevedore and I strewn across my bed as he holds my naked body. Like a father, he tries to soothe me into taking a nap, his strong, gentle hand caressing the gorgeous bloom of knotted African hair that I had back when I was a child—and Juliet enters the room to bring us cold sugary tea and cheese sandwiches. Stevedore cups my breasts with a single warm palm while the other rests in the curve of my hip and he says, "It was when you were born that I began to believe in myself, Eternity. That I could bend the universe."

"But you don't believe in anything," Dr. Juliet reminds him, sweetly.

Then later, after we have eaten the sandwiches and drunk our tea, Juliet lies down with us, her sigh on my forehead and one of her arms caressing my skin as she whisper-sings a lullaby, the sincerity of her voice carrying me at last into a babylike comfort zone; and in that moment of heavenly drowsiness, I look up at the porcelain white skin on Juliet's throat and notice for the first time the thin slash of pink scar tissue that runs across it like a vague pencil mark. You must pay careful attention to what I am telling you: this vague pink mark across her throat, this is where Stevedore once made an incision and removed the Adam's apple before they were married.

It's not a big deal to me. I am used to Dr. Juliet. She has always been my mother—jotting on clipboards, politely stare-smiling, hiding. And even though she now talks on and on in this dungeon, I can still hear her softly singing the lullaby, "*And if that robin bird don't sing, mother's gonna buy you a diamond ring . . .*"

"Who do you think killed Stevedore?" Dr. Juliet asks me. But in her blue eyes he's not dead. I still see the three of us on my childhood bed, the three of us entwined, fast asleep. And then, moments later, she says, "I had nothing to do with the operation he performed on Lucky."

Lucky was our pet orangutan at Africa Farms AIDS Clinic when I was ten or eleven. She'd been there for years, a friendly, trustworthy animal, dragging her arms on the floors as she wobbled down the hallways, her body tilting side to side, carrying faxed documents for the scientists or bringing them a syringe or a thermos of broth for a patient. But one day she just snapped. Grabbed a baseball bat and began wrecking the lab and beating Stevedore with it. In fact, Stevedore would've been killed if Dr. Gobi Kadir, our scientist from India, hadn't unloaded a shotgun into Lucky's backside.

"It was because of a growth on her brain," Dr. Quicken informed us all days later. "Chronic painful brain spasms caused poor Lucky to become delusional and violent."

But the Ajowan and Oluchi people out in the forest and down by the river—they shook their heads when I told them that.

"Lucky was a boy orangutan when they first got him," insisted the tar-black and deep-chocolate faces at the river. "But your father is like God. For his amuse-ment, he switches the animals around—*down there!*" And then, just as one of the blackest faces was about to tell me something, something that she looked as though she'd been dying to tell me since back when I was just a baby and my "parents" Stevedore and Dr. Juliet had first put me in the arms of the river people and asked them to teach me how to be African, her husband stepped up, com-manding, "Sifu-siffo!" And she not only shut up, but from then on, whenever in my presence, was shut up for good.

"Sifu-siffo" (She's lived with whites for more than two days).

And because of that, there were several times when the Ajowans and Oluchi would wait until I was skipping back to the clinic before indulging in their ritual of sit-ting around telling each other stuff. I or anything else touched by whites wasn't to be trusted.

Right now I long to ask them, *Who do you think killed Stevedore?* But Dr. Juliet is busy in the dungeon, telling me stuff. Insisting, "When he cloned you, Eternity, it was the beginning, back when Stevedore and I were newly married and so deep in love. Making you was like bringing a child into the world for us. It was our pas-sion, and though some of the other scientists like Dr. Quicken had already cloned Africans successfully, you were Stevedore's first. And you're well aware that it isn't possible for me to . . . make a baby. When you were Ori-sha, the dead Ajowan woman lying on the observation table, I knew that you would make a beautiful daughter. I wanted you even more than Stevedore . . . I wanted you to exist."

Orisha. Oh God. *Orisha.*

Juliet touches my face so lovingly, yet the butterflies in my stomach seem to suffocate and thicken my urine until it is heavy in my bladder like syrup and straw. I don't feel like a human being anymore.

When you were . . . Orisha.

I struggle to say it, my first-life name . . . Orisha. For some reason, I can't get it to form in my lungs, let alone rise in my throat or fall from my lips. Fresh tears fill my eyes and I can't stop blinking, because Dr. Juliet is crying now. Telling me that I must let go of the rage, disbelief, and bitterness that has consumed my entire being since a few days ago when she first told me what I am.

She is saying, "You shouldn't hate your father, Eternity. He was a good man. He created us. With his bare hands, his mind, his heart, and his imagination, he created us. We are a family, because he loved us."

And as sick as it is, I realize that Dr. Juliet, my mother, is right. This is who we are, and this is our truth. Thanks to Stevedore and his brilliant, lavish way of loving. And I am numb because I fear that no man will ever possess me that way again—first as my father, then as my lover. Loving me like that, literally into being.

"Your visiting time is up!" shouts a uniformed policeman walking through the dungeon with a torch raised above his coal-black arm.

"Accept it!" Juliet urges, squeezing me passionately. "Accept life."

"I'm starting to."

"Good," she says, letting me go. "I'll be back to fetch you in the morning. I'll have Fergie draw you a hot bath and fix us a hearty breakfast. And remember, there'll be some questions by an investigator."

When it looks as though Juliet is about to turn and walk away, I throw my head back like a child in a fit of silent, voiceless wailing, and the gurgling in my throat and the contortions of my crying face temporarily stop her in her tracks.

Since there's nothing she can do until morning, and since she knows that my falling to pieces has little to do with being in jail, she tells me the truth: "This is life, Eternity. None of us anywhere are free."

AFRICA FARMS AIDS CLINIC

None of us anywhere.

Our maid, Fergie, gently awakens me and I notice that I'm in my bed at the clinic and that it's very dark outside. I remember earlier that morning, seeing my name written on the prison clipboard—*Eternity Frankenheimer*—and then my jet-black fingers jotting my signature next to it.

"You're free to go," the guard had said while staring in astonishment that I could actually write my name. He certainly couldn't write his.

I remember that an investigator had come by to see me but that I simply hadn't been able to stay awake after bathing and eating breakfast, because I couldn't sleep at the prison. Dr. Juliet promised him that he could come and see me in the evening if he absolutely had to question me about Stevedore's death.

So now he is downstairs.

"His name is Detective Bekki Diallo," Fergie whispers as she wipes my eyes and mouth with a warm washcloth. Coming out of the dream world, my gaze searches the room for the things that frightened me most as a child. But then I reassure myself that there are no dolls in my room, or perhaps even in the clinic, because Fergie has locked them all away where they can't stare at me.

I yawn powerfully because I'm well rested and then there I am . . . standing bare-breasted before the detective in Dr. Quicken's office and wearing my very finest Oluchi floor-length cotton skirt. Predictably, it's my bald scalp that causes him to do a double take, because although he himself is an Ajowan and occasionally sees topless women walking in the city, he is not used to black girls who still uphold our ancestors' ritual of femininity—the shaving and painting of the female head.

I bow gracefully and say to him, "Koto beddi papa" (Welcome, sir), but he does not respond in kind. In fact he grimaces, slightly embarrassed, which alarms my instincts and causes me to study him closely.

He is a tall, handsome, well-educated Cassavan, light brown in color on his neck and hands—but discolored in the face, especially in the center where it's peeling. His complexion looks unnatural, and within seconds I realize he's a bleacher. One of those modern city-dwellers in our country who uses fade creams to bleach their skin lighter—and what's even more pitiful is that with his pecan-colored flesh, he's already very light complexioned in comparison to most West Africans. But alas . . . even light brown obviously isn't good enough. As he talks, I realize from the faint blue film across his gums that he's also a swallower—a city black who swallows daily what our young people have nicknamed the "Michael Jackson pill," a pill that's supposed to make you turn white, provided you take it long enough. But since no one's turned white yet, we don't actually know how long that is.

I grin, trying not to laugh as I notice his hair. Jungle-kinky at the base but the bulk of it slick and straight, resting on his head like a shiny tar cap. It looks so very bizarre on a black man, yet he talks and behaves as though he really does have the "Been-to" hair of a mixed-race or half-caste person. And because I am so exceedingly jet black in color, there is this elitism in his speech and mannerisms that indicates he regards me as inferior.

"So you like sleeping with white men?" he asks.

"Not as much as you wish to be one."

His mouth falls open like a monkey's and the skin on his wide, flat nose cracks and peels all the more. An instant mutual disgust flares between us.

"The science lady claims that you're not a patient, you don't have AIDS."

"No, I don't have AIDS," I answer.

"Did you murder Dr. Stevedore Frankenheimer?"

"No, I didn't."

"No, I didn't . . . *sir*. Call . . . ME . . . sir."

And there in his eyes I can see the words sparkling like sickle fire: *You topless, backward, black-as-night jungle bitch!* I can see his desire to brutally strike me about the face—for being midnight black and for not being in awe of him.

"No . . . I didn't . . . *sir*."

"The Gon-ghossa has already assigned an English-man, Detective Lance Hightower, to investigate the murder of your father. But as a formality, and in my capacity as Detective Hightower's assistant, I am to question you as a matter of record." He begins checking off notes on his clipboard. While writing, he manages to fish out his wallet, remove a paper photograph, and hand it over to me. Bemused, I notice that it's a picture of a pale, fatigued, resolute-looking white woman with a half-caste child sitting on her lap. Without even glancing at me, the detective assumes I'm impressed and announces, "My wife Zelda and my son Simon."

Something about the pale woman and beige-brown child enchants me, but I don't want him to have the satisfaction of knowing. I hand back the photograph. Then to my utter shock, Detective Bekki Diallo addresses me as though he's some loving older brother delivering valuable advice: "It's dangerous for a girl as black and ugly as you are, little sister, to be walking around thinking so much of herself. These Caucasoids raised you like a princess, but look at your skin, you're blacker than Satan. You need to find a husband and have some boy children and stay out of the sun."

My eyes (*black-magic eyes*, Stevedore used to call them) stare up at him, acknowledging that he's stupid. All I want, seriously, is to spit on him. Ratchet up a hunk of snot and just spit it on him, because although my greatest curiosity in life is an African man who actually lives in a city—I hate this one.

"It says here that you've recently auditioned for the starring role in a film," he adds.

I nod. My stomach fills with dread at the remembrance of what it was that triggered Juliet to reveal to me that I'm a clone—the auditions that Stevedore had me undergo for the lead role in the film biography that the Americans had come to our nation to make—*The Racist*.

It was Stevedore's dream that I be cast as Orisha—
the Ajowan mother who is kicked to death in the streets
of DakCrete for trying to get the young people to stop
swallowing skin-lightening pills and bleaching themselves. In fact, as the script explains, this is the reason
the young Africans have nicknamed Mother Orisha "The
Racist"—because how dare she question their reasons
for wanting to be brighter, and how dare she hand out
pamphlets from health officials decreeing the epidemics
of kidney failure, skin cancer, and liver disease that are
so obviously the result of the skin-lightening agents? It is
Mother Orisha's black womb and preaching black gums
that stand between them and their dream of achieving
a better life, a more successful existence. One in which
their color in this white man's world will no longer
matter—because they won't have any color.

"Keeeel dat racist witch!" the African children chant
as Fanta bottles and rocks fly against Orisha's head. One
of her eyeballs is gouged out; bones resist but crack like
celery; skin is pounded apart like yam—they pelt her
slender tallness with a hate so vicious it crushes consciousness. How dare she judge them? How dare she acknowledge their embarrassment about their coloring? I
can almost remember feeling it, and even more clear is
Stevedore's voice, his gaze entering my head mysteri-
ously as he assures me, "You, Eternity, were *born* to play
this part."

Of course, I hadn't known what he'd meant by such
a curious, passionate announcement, but I was her all
right. And what a masterstroke it would be for him as
creator to watch the actual clone of this slain activist
portray her very life over again. His tongue and what I

think of as his hard, beautiful Richie Cunningham penis enter me at the same time. And there in the darkness, it's as if my girl-cave is a lavish cathedral, like the kind Juliet used to make him go to on Sundays in the city to give confession—only it's me now that he's inside of, confessing to. My pussy is his church.

"This is what I'm talking about," the detective warns me, suddenly. "Why on earth would some Negroid-faced girl from the Oluchi region be trying to humiliate herself with silly dreams of becoming the star of a major Hollywood film? It's affected you negatively—being raised by Caucasoids. You think too much of yourself."

Stung deeply, but not the least bit irrational, I inform him that I've appeared in dozens of films. Stevedore made countless movies using his own equipment, and in every single one that Father made, I, Eternity Frankenheimer, am the star. If he likes, the detective can go out to storage room A-11 and view the cans of celluloid and even get one of the scientists to screen them on the wall in the clinic cafeteria.

He ignores this information, but at last gets to the point. "I could help you, you know." I hadn't expected it, but he jumps right in, his clouded eyes casting me as a stain. "The Michael Jackson pill is difficult to purchase since they made the new antibleaching laws in West Cassavaland and Senegal; not everyone can afford it. Unless you know someone with connections, you get overcharged and your usage gets interrupted. But I've got unlimited access to a regular supply straight from Europe. That's where they make it, you know. *Kindis-Europa* (Magnificent Europe). I can get you Nadinola skin-bleaching cream from Canada and Mexico, and wigs and human hair from Korea too. I could keep you supplied with all that."

In his eyes I see young black schoolgirls and desperate housewives of DakCrete giving him sex in exchange for these products. "What about Percy Commey?" I ask him, and as I say that name, it's as if I've placed burning coals beneath his feet. Percy Obliteri Commey, of course, is the celebrated Ghanaian boxer who made international headlines in 2001 when the right side of his face literally fell apart during a boxing match because of his chronic use of skin-bleaching agents. One small cut on Commey's cheek, courtesy of his opponent, had progressed during the match into small skin-cracks around his nostrils, and then another cut at his right ear, until all the skin on his right side began peeling off before the whole world like a bleeding black mask. Not only did Commey lose his National Super Featherweight belt when it was discovered by the boxing league that he was a bleacher, but also the respect of the West African people, including those who were fellow bleachers and swallowers, because along with the shame of being a national figure caught bleaching, he had also brought his sexuality into question by entering the boxing ring wearing a Jheri-Curl (niggerlox).

"And don't forget about our region's own Wife of Tarzan. She died trying to become Fanta-colored," I remind him to rub it in.

At last he is silenced, because not only have I raised the names of shame, but I've finally convinced him that the glints in my black-magic eyes represent not envy or exasperation over his white wife and half-caste child, but rejection and contempt. To me, he's just another well-dressed, high-up Pogo-nigger who wishes to someday wake up white, even if it's through his grandchildren.

And for that—*he slaps me!* His whole big hand, hard and loud across my face like thunder.

"Ouuuuuheeee!" I scream at the painful sting. My hands hold the right side of my head, and my eyes immediately flood with so many tears they look like stars.

"Eternity!?" shrieks Dr. Juliet from another room, and then she's busting through the door. "Eternity!?"

I am bent over and sobbing. Detective Diallo turns on Dr. Juliet, shouting belligerently, "What kind of child hasn't the manners to respect the positions of men?"

"Yes sir," Dr. Juliet snaps back at him, angrily. Her hands, I think to myself, are as big as any man's, but still they're very gentle and I've never once seen her use them in a fight. She orders him, "Please leave us now."

"You're lucky you haven't been assigned to be the killer," he tells me. "Any dark child will do. And you, scientist—teach this black jungle bitch some respect!" He yells at us as though we're Oluchi tribal wives who've dropped his pan bread in the ashes, his stinging hand clutched into a fist with which he wishes to bash us both. Then he storms out.

"What happened?" Dr. Juliet asks me.

"I didn't want to be light-skinned," I tell her.

WIFE OF TARZAN

Seeing the moon outside my window makes me feel cursed now that I know how I was brought back into the world. I glimpse its full whiteness, the spectral glow of its pearly emulsion embracing my stricken stare like sadness absolute. I tell Fergie, "Close the curtains, please."

And as she blocks out the moon and its whiteness, I take the damp cloth away from my still-stinging cheek, lay it on the nightstand, and turn up my palms to gaze in wonder at the slits on my wrists, barely mended as it's now been only four days since my initial suicide attempt.

I want only to open the earth (my wrists) and be held by Stevedore. But he has already saved me from my suicide attempt. I am alive, and just yesterday he died; yet like a grown man bound and gagged in a tiny wooden box, I feel the new life that he put inside me kicking from within, the voice of its white father lamenting bitterly: *Ife kwulu ife akwudebe ya* (If one thing stands, another thing stands by it). He is referring to our clinic's philosophy that happenstance and synchronicity order matter; not coincidence. This is why I can't help but wonder about Detective Diallo and what it's like to actually bleach one's skin and swallow pills and hate one's own flesh—not his *being*, but his flesh—to literally spit curses from the eye of his penis in the hope of erasing his own people.

I wonder in confusion about our nation's "Poem of Patriotism," words erected by proud African men on that day of our people's independence: *For we are the Africans . . . the children of the earth's first garden . . . that perfect, deliberate blackness that can only be described as the genesis of vision itself. Let freedom ring.*

"How can he, a black man, just erase us?" I ask as Fergie tucks me in.

My words stop her cold. Her face hardens like a boarded-up wall beneath a cracked mirror. In shame's fleeting shadows, the door of privacy within her stare makes it obvious that she has more in common with Detective Diallo than with me. It startles me into a chill.

"Fergie?"

She whispers into my ear, conspiratorially, "Beautiful people owned us, and that's how we found out that we were the damned."

"Beautiful people?"

"Angel's food cake is white, devil's food cake is black. You never noticed that? I believe it's because God loves his white children more than he loves his half-castes . . . and he loves his half-castes more than he loves us black ones. Otherwise, why would he let them conquer us and colonize and enslave us and have nothing but good riches to show for it? The white man took us off the dirt roads and put us on buses. He put shoes on our feet and created airplanes so that we could fly. He invented cameras and showed us pictures that only prove how ugly and poor we are. That computer you love because it puts the world at your fingertips—it's from the white man's genius. On all the stamps and money in Africa, you'll notice the face of the white man's mother printed right across it, because that's how much he loves his mother—he wants to see her image everywhere he goes. The whiter she is, the more he loves her. No such tragedy as a white woman being *too* white. But how many African women do you know who can boast that they're not too black? I tell you, God loves the Caucasoid race. I've put ice cubes in the white man's glass and I've put ice cubes in the black man's glass, and it never fails—the white man's ice is colder."

The white man's ice is colder?

Her words pierce my heart as though the syllables

are cells from the AIDS virus, and though I've already died and left this earth in a past life for trying to glorify my people's darkness, the truth confronts me now that this is what the martyr gets—*nothing*. I have been erased and I am back and nothing has changed. And as her words suffocate my soul, it's the knowledge that nothing has changed that makes me long for an endless sleep, a sweet suicide. But Fergie won't shut up. I've set free her bitterness; her impassioned whisper splashes forth, "It's the young insecure ones like you who think it's a tragedy to be ugly, but you're wrong. Women like me understand that we don't need beauty—because Jesus loves us. In His blue eyes, by His Father's mercy, we shall be saved."

"The river blacks," I venture, "say that Jesus was a black man, an African."

"That's because they're ignorant. If Jesus was black, why would black people be swallowing a pill to make them white and straightening their hair to be like Christ? For all and sundry, he was white—and someday, when I cross over, I shall be white and blue-eyed too. I've told all my children and all my grandchildren and all my great-grandchildren that when Jesus comes back for us, we're going to walk in the light. Praise God, the feet of sweet Jesus. Praise His goodness and mercy."

When tears come to Fergie's eyes, because she so pitifully longs for that colorless day of acceptance, unconditional love, and inclusion, I feel compelled to spit in her round mud-colored face. Of course, I don't dare. But I bring up something that for her kind is worse than spitting in her face.

"Do you remember the Wife of Tarzan?" I ask.

"She doesn't count!" Fergie snaps dismissively. "Why are you always bringing up dead people? And not even good dead people!"

Patiently, I remind her that the Wife of Tarzan was not originally a human being, but a toxic poison invented by Stevedore to ward off the giant waterbugs that used to rise up out of the jungle after heavy rains and swarm our clinic's compound. I inform her, as Stevedore had informed me back when he was perfecting the recipe for the poison, that in ancient Rome and Greece, the upper-middle-class women had achieved the illusion of being extremely white-skinned by wearing a heavy acetate foundation, a makeup created by dissolving lead shavings into vinegar, and that the consequence of wearing it was that after years of exposure, they developed brain disorders such as dementia, chronic migraine headaches, severe memory loss, and sometimes even blindness. Nevertheless, Stevedore had pointed out, the women still did anything they could to be as white as possible, because in those ancient Roman and Greek societies, whiteness was the sole marker of status, respectability, and moral fortitude, and only the royal and governing classes had been really, truly, fully white.

I then explain to Fergie that in our own West Cassavaland hillside there existed a similar ancient makeup, but a natural one, tekur mud—a bluish charcoal clay that West African kings routinely melted to darken their penises with, and that queens wore to assert higher status by transforming their midnight-black faces into even darker, smoother complexions, over which they would paint intricate patterns of white dots and drape their shaven heads with cowry shells and other jewelry, all of it to achieve maximum "Nyama" (black as all black put together), a state of precolonial being that denoted femininity in women and fertility for African royals. But, alas, tekur mud also brought on madness, elephantitis of the scrotum, diabetes, and blindness, and it was out of boredom and curiosity that Stevedore had mixed the lead acetate Roman-Greek formula with the African tekur mud and melted it down with lye, brine of sericin (silk gum), and water to create what he called Wife of Tarzan, the poison of the Gods. I remind Fergie that its main virtue for all of us living at the compound was that it was odorless and therefore the perfect insect repellent—especially since the jungle's waterbugs often grow as big as lobsters and can run as fast as the pregnant bush rats.

She remembers now, this lethal, odorless poison that we all appreciated so much—until, of course, its name became the epitaph of a young woman.

"Dr. Juliet killed her!" Fergie whispers with a grave, blunt decree. "Just like she murdered that white father of yours—who you marked . . . like a lioness. The girl was a prostitute!"

"Only because her parents forced her!"

"Do not speak the unspeakable," Fergie warns me. "There are certain things that decent Africans do not ever discuss, even amongst one another."

But spying the stitches in my wrists, I realize now that it's *time*—time to have no more secrets, at least not the ones that are forced upon us. And just as I think it, I imagine our lovely Wife of Tarzan come stumbling out of the bush as though she's still alive.

Her name had been Aneela and she'd come from a moderately well-to-do middle-class family in the Tenuba Valley, the Woluti-Zombas. Like neighboring Senegal, West Cassavaland had legalized prostitution in the late 1960s. As a consequence, there became a strange phenomenon among the families of the African upper class—the legal registering of their very darkest-skinned daughters as prostitutes in the men's sporting ranches that catered sexual booty along the resort coastline and in DakCrete. Aneela was only sixteen when her lawyer father and schoolteacher mother awakened her from a deep sleep one night, the mother binding her hands and covering her mouth while the father gently and robotically, but lovingly, took her virginity, after which they registered her with the state as a Career Girl, Title C, and posited her at the Air Force men's club, explaining to the teenager that the sacrifice she was about to make was the most noble thing in the world—and that because of her earnings, the family would now be able to keep her two older brothers in college in England. They told Aneela that this was, in all discretion, a typical and honorable practice in several African countries, which it is, and that neither of her two slightly older sisters could go in her place, because like their mother, they had been born the color of peanut butter and would surely fetch fat marriage dowries for the family bank, and therefore were already in training as Needed Wifery.

Right after losing her virginity, Aneela tried to hug her mother. But the mother, the same mother who had held her down so that she could be raped by her father, only flinched away, uttering the rebuke, "Don't touch me." Her demeanor toward her own child was one of setting out the trash; and naturally, in that moment, Aneela was transformed into a kind of monster more tragic than any prostitute. "You," the African mother had whispered, "came out looking like your father and your brothers. Jet black—with hair that doesn't grow."

"They really work. I'm lighter," Aneela tells me years later when we're in the clinic's den watching Stevedore's videotapes of *Happy Days*. In her palm I see the pretty cream-colored pills and the faint blue film lining her gums from years of toxic buildup—and then I cringe, wondering as I watch her ingest them if they taste anything like the creamy drops of semen that she enjoys swallowing right out of Stevedore's penis, her willingness to do it being the reason that he hides her in our clinic, nevermind that she's registered to the Air Force men's club, a prostitute without AIDS living in and working out of an AIDS clinic. And, of course, most baffling of all is that she has such a stunningly beautiful dark-chocolate complexion, considerably lighter than my charcoal coloring, and that even with her round princess face and gazellelike eyes, she considers herself deformed and needful of erasure.

A few weeks later she dies by accident after Juliet jokingly tells her that the mysterious thermoses in our injections refrigerator that have POISON—DO NOT DRINK written across them in bold letters are in fact filled with the secret formula that caused Michael Jackson to fade from black to white. I tell Aneela not to believe it, that Juliet's just teasing her, and that it's actually a poison Stevedore calls Wife of Tarzan—but she gets up in the middle of the night, a whole weft from her poorly sewn hair weave clinging to her pillow, and swallows down the grayish-white death milk anyway.

At the Wife of Tarzan's clinic-sponsored funeral, I notice that so many of the city Africans who have come to mourn her have their own faint blue gums and peeling Nadinola-covered faces. Skeletal hands are draped habitually over the spot on their torsos where their kidneys ache, and it occurs to me that no matter how many thousands of AIDS-infected black bodies I've seen piled up by the authorities and torch-burned out of this world, AIDS is not the only disease killing off an entire race of people.

The Racist

Suddenly, I remember who killed Stevedore. I'm afraid to tell Dr. Juliet who took him away from us—she wouldn't believe me! But as I think back to the casting of the film the Americans made, every explicit detail of my father's death crawls back to me.

This is right before I frightened Juliet into telling me that I'm a clone, it's right before my monthlies stopped coming, it's right before I discovered that the reason I felt so haunted by the passion of Orisha after studying her and screen testing to play her in the film was because I had actually been her in a previous life. It's right before I slit my wrists.

It is the night in which I am having a dream, only days before I discover I'm a clone; I will then know that it wasn't actually a dream, but rather a memory. In the dream, I am a young Ajowan girl of around thirteen. My mother's blue-black arm is pulling me behind her and we are entering a movie house on a dusty red clay avenue in DakCrete. You must take note that in the dream-memory it's 1969, just one year after our nation's independence from Great Britain. For the first time, the seats inside are filled with black African people—Oluchis, Ajowans, Mandingos, Ashanti, Wolofs, Hausa-mon, Yorubans, Igbo, and the "pot liquor" (city-stock mixtures of blacks, chocolates, and purples). We are, indeed, a theater full of common people. Then, suddenly, up on the screen, out of total darkness come the first images of this film that purports to tell the story of one of West Cassavaland's greatest ancestors—our beloved Mother Iyanla. But instead of applause, an audible gasp of shock ripples through the audience.

The actress on screen is the color of a yam's yellow innards, her nose pepper-shaped rather than flat, wide, and sexy like a West African's. Her lips are juicy, but not as everlasting as ours. She is not us, but rather an echo of us, a watered-down Europeanized imitation of our mother's essence—and sure enough, some skinny nappy-headed African in the front row immediately jumps up and shouts at the screen, "That's not our mother!"

"Oh, sit the hell down," responds a group of men—slick chocolate ones from the upper ranks—and that of course stokes the hurt feelings and betrayal that the African women in the audience will come to almost always experience when they sit through movies made about them by Western men. On screen, the insult against our mother seed continues issuing itself as the husband is shown to be a very dark-skinned West Cassavan, and the children, miraculously, even darker and more "us-looking" than the father. Only the mother has been whitened and watered down, and as the audience bristles heatedly, one of the Mandingo sons at midrow yells out, "Without our real mother, we cannot be born!"

"Silence, black boy!" shouts a slick chocolate man.

But then a Yoruba wife jumps up and demands, "How can we sit and watch this colonialist donkey shit? They could have at least cast a woman who goes with the landscape!"

"Without our real mother, we cannot be born!" calls an Ashanti man from the back, and it turns into a riot. Bottles fly across the theater, people are up on their feet hissing and cursing at the yellow woman on the screen.

"Without our real mother, we cannot be born!" the Africans of 1969 chant with rage.

And as my own mother hurriedly pulls my siblings and me out of the theater's pandemonium and into the hot sun, I immediately notice a skeletal dog coming up the street with a human arm in its mouth, a Dalmatian I think at first. But as it gets closer, I realize it's just a mutt, and it's right then that a green bottle hits me upside the head—waking me from the dream—and there we are, Stevedore and I, entering the sound stage where they'll soon begin shooting *The Racist*, where I've been astounding the production crew with my auditions for the role of Orisha for weeks now.

Strangely and ominously, they applaud as I enter stage B-12. Some of the African members of the production crew shout out, "You *are* Orisha—in the flesh!" But as they're clapping and saying these things for only God knows why, I glance over at the director's chair and standing behind it is a tall, slender, elegant biracial girl possessing honey-pineapple fashion-model good looks. Her head is hooded by a fedora and her eyes fasten to mines with an apologetic nervousness. I know instantly that this is the mutt with my arm in its mouth. She has been brought all the way to Africa to play the role of

Orisha—to erase any memory of the real me.

Suddenly I taste my color. In prepublicity releases, the American studio claimed to have chosen to shoot the film in Africa because they wanted authenticity. They said they wanted to cast the female equivalent of Dji-mon Hounsou—a girl who really looks the part.

"What the hell is going on?" Stevedore demands as one of the film's black American producers comes running up. He thanklessly informs us that the studio in California received a call from their financial backers in New York and London. "They loved your screen tests, Eternity—they couldn't get over how much you actually resemble the real-life Orisha. But they don't think American moviegoers are ready for your look."

My look, mind you, is not chocolate like Lauryn Hill, Whoopi Goldberg, or Naomi Campbell—it is pitch black and shimmering like the purple outer space of the universe. I am the charcoal that creates diamonds. I am the *blackest* black woman.

"You could at least cast a woman who goes with the African landscape!" Stevedore snaps as he too notices the mixed-race actress standing behind the director's chair.

"The part of Orisha has been rewritten," coughs the producer. "She's now the biracial daughter of a British naval officer and an African princess."

"But Orisha was a pure Ajowan!" Stevedore protests, emphatically. "A real-life blue-black Ajowan woman who died fighting against skin lightening—and now you go and lighten her skin for the movie!"

"I'm sorry, Dr. Frankenheimer, but our orders come from Hollywood."

Haw-*lee*-wood.

On the ride home, I am silent and sick to my stomach. I've basically just been told that although I look exactly like Orisha and gave a riveting performance, I'm too black to play her in a film. A beautiful African woman can't possibly be charcoal. Even deeper than that is the implicit message that my African features are deformed and my bald head is a joke. I am no longer my people's real mother. For that lie, I hate the world. I feel the activist Orisha still inside me. And because of that message I need to have sex immediately, as passionately as possible.

I make Stevedore pull over to the side of the road—I need my skin touched and my features kissed and my smooth skull massaged. Only by human touch can this denigration of my body be healed back to wellness—but just as soon as Stevedore's lovemaking reassures me of my human form's normalness and desirability, Dr. Juliet snatches away my humanity altogether.

I tell her I didn't get the part, but she doesn't give a shit. She's edgy and upset because I still haven't had my monthly.

"If you're pregnant by my husband, Eternity, then we need to begin thinking about an abortion right away."

An abortion? I shake my head. The Oluchi river women have raised me with the belief that abortion for African women is evil and wrong.

"Sleeping with your father is one thing," Juliet continues, "but I won't have you giving him children. And besides, your first semester at university is coming up. You can't attend an English school pregnant." She is hurting inside like a wounded animal and unable to control her rage. "I can't be reminded of your betrayal on a daily basis by having this child loitering round the premises!"

"I didn't betray you! I didn't know it was wrong!"

"I am your mother! Why are you loyal to Stevedore but not to me? I helped make you in that goddamn lab!"

The words seem ridiculous: *I helped make you in that goddamn lab.* But as her blue eyes turn jagged, darkening as though filled with blood and fog, I can see that this is what she's been dying to say for years. Her heart is sliced in pieces by Stevedore's fornication. She wants to cut me, get inside me, wound me back.

"You were *made!*" she says. "You were engineered. Didn't we teach you not to believe in coincidence? No one left you on the goddamn doorstep! You're one of your father's science projects. You're a fucking clone . . . *a clone!*"

Her words are insanity—hilarious, cruel, and hurtful.

Yet I know it must be true after living all my life with Stevedore and Juliet. The signs have all been there. The shock of it causes me to vomit in disbelief. "How could you!"

It suddenly all makes sense: the Africans neighboring the clinic have always regarded me as an outsider and hidden their conversations from me. I can't help but wonder whether or not I have a soul. Then Juliet reveals that it's from Orisha, "The Racist" herself, that I am cloned. That's too much. I faint.

"Do you hate him now?" Dr. Juliet asks when I come to. I can tell in her bitter, blank eyes that she hopes I hate him. "Do you hate your father now that you know it's because of him you're knocked up like a plantation wench and don't have a soul? He violated your DNA, engineered you, fucked you—took your soul."

I've lost something after fainting. I can't speak. I can barely fathom my nothingness. I am shattered.

"You'd better not tell anybody about what you are or what he did," Juliet hisses. Lab business will continue as usual, she says. "The World CDC Federation has laws against cloning. Africa Farms could be shut down and Stevedore imprisoned for the rest of his life if this gets out."

Come midnight I slit my wrists.

I LOVE RICHIE CUNNINGHAM

Stevedore threatens to kill Dr. Juliet for telling me what I am. He tends my wrists and puts the whole clinic staff on vigil around me. But I can't tolerate being in the same room with him. He has to go.

I coil in fetal position pregnant with his child.

I regret that I survived the suicide attempt.

I strain to remember when I was dead. The whole world is chilling madness. I'm not myself, yet I have the knowledge of two selves. I am not a coincidence, yet it turns out I am just as much an oddity as my monstrous parents. I am beautiful, yet after being told I'm too black to play myself in a film, I now know that beauty, like race, is a social construct—and it's evil. I know that black people and white people both are Satan's pride. Stevedore has always joked that "trust" is when two cannibals can give each other a blowjob. He finds that cute. He says he wants this baby.

I want out.

"Our child," Stevedore predicts as he holds my face in his hands after kissing me in the clinic hallway, "will be born with nice hair and a good color."

He lifts my chin, staring into my black-magic eyes, and says, "All my life, I've really wanted to love some-one, Eternity—to have someone I can completely trust. That's why it was necessary. Hours in the lab creating you put love inside me."

"But you're not God, Stevedore! You had no right!"

"Of course I'm God," he jokes. "I'm a white man!"

And it's because of this small joke, you see, this tiny joke that actually has enough truth in it to be funny, that I decide the only way for me to own myself is to drink the Wife of Tarzan. This time, the suicide will give me relief. And just an hour later, even with my barely healed wrists stinging against the pull, I open the refrigerator where we keep the thermoses marked POISON—DO NOT DRINK.

I ignore Stevedore's voice calling from outdoors. He is working in the hot African sun, his white flesh burn-ing redder and redder, unaware that the baby and I are about to die.

Playing in my mind is the melody from that movie the scientists made me watch all my life—The Wizard of Oz. It's the one where the Scarecrow sings, "If I only had a brain." And now, opening the thermos, I think of the Scarecrow, the Tin Man, the Cowardly Lion, and my mother—Dr. Juliet. It seems that after death I have come back as the very thing that always scared me as a little girl—a doll. In fact, there's no denying any longer that I'm a doll somebody made, which must be why I fear them so insanely. And so I begin to hum the Scarecrow's melody, only I change the words and sing, *"If I only had a soul."*

Stevedore thinks he's God. But I intend for him to feel my power when he walks back in the clinic and finds me and the fetus dead. Yes, Father—I will show you God.

Topless in a flowing kente skirt, I pour myself a glass of rice milk and mix the Wife of Tarzan in with it. I drift out of the kitchen, sailing room to room as though sleepwalking. Then I stand there, bracing my mind and body for that moment when I will drink the poison and leave this damnable earth and all its misery behind. But just as life would have it—the unexpected—Stevedore comes into the room, his ice-cream flesh dripping from the heat and his burnt red arm wiping away the sweat on his forehead.

"God, it's hot," he says—and he takes my drink.

He comments that I look breathtaking with my breasts *out like that*—and he cradles the glass of poison with a desire to quench his burning thirst.

What a coincidence!

Stevedore: my creator, father, lover.

And as I watch him lifting the glass to his lips, the seconds moving slower than a snail, I close my eyes to happenstance and synchronicity, to God . . . and to all eternity.

I Have an Awful Lot to Hide

Years after my father's poisoning, I am amazed to be alive and free. Airbrushed with a glossy enthusiasm, my face is plastered all over the world on billboards sixty feet high. But somehow, no matter the competition I'm giving Naomi Campbell, Christy Turlington, and Claudia Schiffer, I still secretly regard myself as a monster.

I've just arrived back in West Cassavaland for a vacation and I have the most fascinating man in my sights. I still don't have a lot of experience with men, so I stare quietly.

The city dwellers, who in DakCrete are mostly Christian, warn me all the time, "You need Jesus." They don't know anything about my pretty little biracial daughter I named Hope, or about how I was kicked to death by Pogo-nigger skin bleachers and then resurrected, or how exactly I got to be so rich and beautiful. But whenever they see me dancing in the club with my white man or shopping along Gold Acre Boulevard or purchasing yams at market, they either give me a look that says it or they plain say it with their mouths, "YOU . . . NEED . . . JESUS."

And as I watch him now—our nation's internationally acclaimed messiah of rap music and big talk, King Sea Horse Twee—rise up naked from a clear blue lagoon, I think about the fact that my body, which has quickly become one of the most photographed bodies in the world, has not yet been penetrated by a black man's penis. That being penetrated by a black man's penis (a *city-dwelling* black man's penis) is the one thing I've longed for and fantasized about for most of my life—even more than being blessed by God.

"The afternoon's coconut wine," my personal hotel servant announces as he sets down my drink, bows, and then shoots away without us ever making eye contact, my bony hand lifting and turning over the cover of the latest edition of *Vogue Europe*, upon which they've posed me—*Supermodel Eternity Frankenheimer*, it says—as some unbelievably perfect goddess; the handlebar cheekbones of my charcoal face peering out aristocratically as my flexible curves imitate the letter S; my wrists slave-chained yet clasped to my hips in chic defiance; scarab beetles made of solid gold pressed upon my fingers like honeycomb; my naked, living breasts sprayed a shimmering silver; my hair weaved into the thick, wild lion's mane of an Ethiopian woman. Yes, I turn the cover down because should the rap star bounce over, I don't wish to mislead him.

For days now, Mr. Twee and I have been stealing glances at one another, whispering questions in the ears of our servants and lackeys, nodding polite hellos and dutifully embossing our celebrity—but upon seeing him arise from the lagoon, bare as though newly born from a vat of chocolate, I feel most assuredly that we aren't going to leave this paradise until we pass something *fragile* (to be a polite African lady) between the two of us.

He runs a hand over the sexy stubble of his closely shaven head and arches his shoulders in such a way that all the muscles in his limbs and torso flex and tense, glistening in the sun like a great athlete's body, so that his large penis and heavy-hanging balls overflow the cusp of his other hand, as he latches onto my gaze like a shaman intent on taming a cobra.

I purse my lips together and glance away in defer-ence to a curiosity that is ancient and idyllic, rooted like an ancestor between us. And, you have to understand, because we are both famous blacks with big egos and reputations to protect—and because famous egotistical blacks are so insecure and fearful of rejection, especially rejection from one's own kind—it's just better, I believe, if we don't complicate these days of heaven, especially since we've come to this resort to be languid, stress-free, and lazy in an African seaside paradise that traditionally caters to rich whites. And because M magazine is doing a profile on me and watching every little thing I do. But I won't lie. Sweet lonely Jesus knows that we want to . . . *be animals together*. We both act like we're bothered by it.

As King Sea Horse strolls into the shade of the massive palm trees, the perfect chocolate cheeks of his masterful buttocks flexing helmetlike as he kneels down to chat with one of three wives he keeps around the world—this one being Millicent York, a young white English feminist magazine writer who originally criticized the misogyny in his lyrics and called him a "hip-hop brute"—I think about the other day when government soldiers came barging into the resort to arrest him. Cuffing him and shoving him around in public for everyone to see before they escorted him to Spy Control at the local army base and detained and interrogated him for three days about his latest CD, *Tarzan Was My Bitch!*, and about his comments to foreign newspapers regarding the upcoming elections and his reputed pot smoking.

I think about his handsome rude-boy face splashed

across the front of the newspapers the day after his arrest and my mother, Dr. Juliet, phoning me all the way from Africa Farms to ask if I was still vacationing at the Queen Elizabeth Shoreline Resort, and whether or not I knew that West Africa's bad boy of rap music was on the premises as well.

"Yes, mother," I had told Juliet, cheerfully. "We've passed each other quite a bit. He's really cute!"

"Stay away from him, Eternity. That boy's got a death wish. He thinks just because the young people worship him and the Europeans buy that barking rhetoric he calls music that he can say anything he wants about the government and not be killed for it. In fact, with the elections coming up, I'd feel a lot better if you were back in England with James Lord."

"Mother, I'm fine. I haven't even spoken with Sea Horse Twee. He's here with one of his wives."

"He beats women—*beats the shit out of them!*" my mother had said. "Not white ones, just black ones."

"Okay, Mom. I'll steer clear of him. James is returning to London in a few months and I'll go home then. I have shows coming up in Milan and Spain. I won't be in Africa long."

"You'd be wise to stop showing off your money and get out of here!"

"Well, what about you, Mother? Why aren't you leaving?"

"Because I'm white, Eternity!" And then *click*. She was gone and I had busted up laughing. I went back to being intrigued by King Sea Horse's handsome face in the newspapers, the headlines blaring in bold black letters, INSTIGATOR . . . GRASS-SMOKING BIG MOUTH

. . . DO NOT LISTEN TO THIS BOY . . . and to watching a British video cassette of the urgently spicy "dang-boy beat" music videos that, although banned in most of Africa, were making him all the rage on the European rap scene.

Feel Me

"Ten billion in AID—dis no AID—you raped n robbed de Motherland! Your debt can never be paid! BOOSHA!" Sea Horse rapped as his video showed poverty-stricken mobs of African tribes barging into the presidential palace, forcing the government officials (who were stuffing money into their pockets) to get up and jigga-dance. Tombstones bearing their names were placed against their chests while oil refineries waving Saudi, American, and Canadian flags could be seen exploding outside the palace windows. A bikini-clad Mandingo hoochie dancer swung the most bodacious black booty I've ever seen, the words *Mother Africa* written in living dayglow against chocolate-fudge ass cheeks as her gigantic breasts jiggled like warring sea lions. The camera cut back to Sea Horse in time for him to add, *"Pogo-nigger rum . . . is the death of the drum!"*

What?

Two women, one dressed up as Queen Elizabeth and the other as Condoleezza Rice, were depicted running down a shanty dirt road, tripping in heels and losing their wigs.

I couldn't believe what I was seeing.

White, Arab, and Asian members of the United Nations were shown having their toes sucked by a lineup of kneeling African dignitaries. The row of black politi-

cians, one of whom bore a striking resemblance to Kofi
Annan, were shown in close-up as the naked feet of white
men, pink-toed bunions and all, were fully cram-stuffed
into their full-lipped mouths while King Sea Horse Twee
grabbed at his crotch and rapped with a belligerent rage:
"*Pogo-nigger rum . . . is the death of the drum! . . . Pogo-nigger rum
is the FIST in the sun!*"

Then he ripped off his shirt to reveal that chest!
Sweet lonely Jesus!
He struck his fist to the sun and declared:

We need blood! We need war!
We need a bath!
They keep'n score!
BOOSHA!

I stood mesmerized, my trembling mouth chanting
along with the booty-shaking video hoochie: "*Pogo-nigger
rum is the FIST in the sun!*" Before I knew it, my fingers were
popping, my shoulders and hips swinging to the beat,
and even though I'd been raised in a lab by whites and
therefore couldn't dance by black people's standards,
my feet, hands, and booty just wouldn't stop trying. The
Oluchi drums and ululations that Sea Horse had mixed
with hip-hop beats and chant-style rap rituals to create
this new sound called dang-boy beat music was so in-
toxicating that one couldn't help but feel liberated:

We gotta CEASE with the begg'n!
　　　　　Koo-Noo-E-Goo!
We gotta stop with the bleaching!
　　　　　Koo-Noo-E-Goo!

We must rebuke de King Kongs!
                    Koo-Noo-E-Goo!
You need a condom while you preaching!
                    Koo-Noo-E-Goo!

That night, while the real flesh-and-blood King Sea Horse Twee was locked up somewhere being interrogated by West Cassavaland's Spy Control, I watched every pulsating frame of his music videos over and over again, and for the first time since finding out that I'm a clone, I felt as though I had a *soul*. Just like anybody else. Out of that enchanted moment, the most grateful tears ran down my face.

Enter Me

At my dressing table, hours after watching Sea Horse lounge in the shade of the lagoon with his wife, the two of them saying nothing, I sit in the mirror strangely terrified about the upcoming interview with M magazine and beguiled by my own face.

I have an awful lot to hide.

I look into my charcoal face and I see . . . *eternity*—blood-fucked and irrevocable—the whole world being made. I see love, my parent's love, the actual omnipotence of these scientists thoroughly cooked into my flesh, seeping to the bone; a love deeper and lonelier than oceans of sky, a longing so apocalyptic in its naturalness that after the penis of man falls from my lips, their sucking goes trembling into prayer. Pious passionate prayer, because I feel that I am Africa itself—captured, lobotomized, and made over through the domineering dreams of someone else's expectations—Africa, the colonizer's clone, the slave trader's clone, the media's clone. Knowing by fire that nothing ever dies and believing in my heart that beauty is evil—*me and everything within me from both of me*—peering into the looking-glass as my stare wanders at the speed of light over the African landscape, leaping from one village to the next, one jungle-headed child to one river to one pregnant belly to one man and his wife, the laying-down dance, his roots penetrating so deep within her that I imagine her dark body to be the earth itself. And then, just before I end my realization with "Udodo" (Amen), determining that I must hide as much of the real Eternity as I can from the readers of M magazine, my personal hotel servant appears in the doorway with a robe and towel draped in the crook of his arm, his eyes averted so as not to rupture my privacy as he dutifully inquires, "Will Miss Frankenheimer be taking her night swim this evening?"

Exit Me

Because of water, I have the single happiest memory of my life—the baptizing of my sweet little baby daughter, Hope. I see her precious feet kicking excitedly as the chanting Oluchi Nana lowers her into the river that day, our naked breasts numbering in the hundreds under tentacles of hot sun.

During labor, while squatting over the birth pillow as though taking a shit, the mother is allowed to chant, "*Exit me . . . exit me . . . exit me.*"

I remember how much it hurt bringing Hope into the world and yet how good it felt the first time I held her delicate head against my body and watched as she put her thumb in her mouth. I remember Dr. Juliet and our maid Fergie and the Oluchi Nana standing over my bed as I closed my eyes and cursed my whole stupid intellect for those times I'd so much as dared to dream of killing myself and the baby. And even when the word came from Dr. Juliet's Afro Catholics and Fergie's postcolonial Protestants that because I'd given birth to a "good luck" child—not a black baby, mind you, but a half-Caucasoid child—I was now invited to sit at the front of their churches where the pews were usually reserved for mulattoes and brown skins, the middle rows for chocolate fudge–colored, and the very back for the royal-black charcoals. I remember shrugging it off and not being mad, because having Hope beside me erased everyone else.

HOPE

"She looks like Stevedore when she yawns," Dr. Juliet remarked painfully one afternoon.

"Go ahead and cry, Mother. I know you miss him. I do too."

"No time for crying," she replied curtly. "Now that the baby's born, you need to get off to England—to the university. You need to figure out what you're going to do with your life."

I hadn't yet lucked into modeling.

"I'm not leaving Hope, I can tell you that. And I've already said that I'm not going to school either. I'll live off the money Stevedore left me and go swimming every day. I prefer being at the river with the Oluchi people. They have a world too, you know."

"You can't live in this world without papers."

"Mother, I'm not even twenty and I've already been trained and educated to death!"

"Knowledge is the key to everything, Eternity."

"I know that, Juliet!"

Hearing me call her Juliet gave her pause for a moment. "Then what will you do, Eternity? Your inheritance won't last forever, and even if you find a good man, marriage is a transitory affair these days—there's no guaranteed security in it."

"I'm never getting married."

"And why is that?"

"Because I have no soul, Mother!"

"Well, like I told you—you're perfect for academia!"

And on and on it went for several days . . . until one humid afternoon when I was at the riverbank cradling and singing to my sweet Hope and dunking both her feet and my breasts in and out of the water. Suddenly Hope smiled with a huge, clown-scary grin, her eyes turning to glass as they beheld me with the warmest, most chilling sparkle.

"Hope?" I called. But her lips stretched out oddly like a cat's yawn, showing me the entire inside of her mouth and throat, tensing up as though paralyzed—her head cocked to one side like her neck was trying to stretch itself into the letter $\mathcal{Q}$ . . . and I thought that she must be having a seizure!

My breathing became like a cheetah's and I cradled her as gently as I could and ran like a shot to the clinic for help, but by the time my family got her on the examining table and calmed me down—with Dr. Quicken, my mother, Dr. Chomsky, Dr. Yen Foo, and Dr. Gobi Kadir doing everything they could—Hope was seemingly back to normal, her happy feet kicking and her body wiggling as she made gurgling baby sounds and her little hand wrapped around one of my fingers until it was a tiny fist squeezing me with love.

"She's blind," Dr. Quicken informed us, coldly.

I was speechless.

"We need to do X-rays, Eternity. She appears normal right now, but she's gone blind. Look at the bottom of her feet, they're blue, and she's laughing because the vibrations under her skin are tickling her. She thinks it's us playing with her—but it's some kind of abnormality of the nervous system."

I threw my head back and my whole body trembled with sadness. Within that same hour, Hope was dead.

"It was a brain aneurysm," Dr. Quicken would report two days later. "She didn't feel any pain, Eternity. She was asleep."

But on the night that Hope actually died, Dr. Juliet came to my room and, for the first time in my life, I balled up my fist and damn near knocked her clear into next week, outraged with her inhumanity.

"I can clone her, Eternity. I can clone your baby. I can bring you a whole new Hope—"

"NO!" I was horrified. "That's why she was sick in the first place!"

Dr. Juliet cowered against the wall, then her body slumped to the floor.

"Because of something defective inside me, I'm not human! I'm a freak—I'm not even supposed to be here living and breathing right now!"

"No one asks to come into this world, Eternity, none

of us! We feel just like you feel. And stop saying that you're not a human—of course you're a human being! Of course you have a soul! Being a clone simply means that one is a duplicate, an exact replica of one's own self, starting over from scratch. And that's all I was saying about Hope—that she doesn't have to stay gone. We can bring her back!"

Exhausted by the mere reality of my circumstances—the daughter of a white couple from Ohio, with the last name Frankenheimer—I shook my head and cursed God. I refused to look at Dr. Juliet there on the floor. What, after all, do you say to a woman who was born a man and considers her physics books and journals to be Holy Scripture?

"We can clone Hope," she repeated meekly.

"No, Mother—I forbid it. My daughter's dead, leave her that way. This is an AIDS research clinic. Stop playing God with the bodies of the natives! I forbid you to lay a finger on my daughter's DNA!"

I cried uncontrollably that whole night. At some point well past midnight, my mother got up off the floor and lay beside me. She caressed my brow and wiped at my tears and hummed to me, ever-gently, *"And if that robin bird don't sing, Mother's gonna buy you a diamond ring . . ."*

But I missed out on recognizing her defiance. At that time, it never occurred to me to be suspicious about the long hours she spent in the lab, sometimes sleeping there.

STARTING OVER FROM SCRATCH

I came to love my mother so much in those days after

Hope died. Not only did Dr. Juliet let me have my way when I petitioned the Oluchi chief for Hope to be granted a traditional night funeral, she also followed custom and bared herself topless while carrying my daughter's dead body wrapped in kente cloth to Chief Thiogo's compound in DayyWo at the cataract of Oluchi River. Dr. Juliet was white as milk when she left but beet red upon arrival. The Africans laughed, sneered, and stared in disbelief at the sight of a topless white woman placing a dead baby into the stone mouth of the Womo Pillar and chanting in the Oluchi language, "Return to me"—but they did not refuse us a burial ceremony.

In fact, the Oluchi buried my daughter with love. But during the drinking of palm wine afterward, they were rude to Dr. Juliet. One of them called her a man, and that then became the night I chose my white mother over Africa. I vowed never to love the Oluchi people as I had before.

"There's no way they could know about my past," mother insisted back in the clinic as we were fixing ourselves lunch. "It's because I'm a white woman, Eternity—and a scientist. Don't forget how they always held that against Stevedore. The civilized Africans in the cities love medicine and training, but these rural naked ones . . ."

I decided to ask her something I had never before worked up the courage to ask—and not because I didn't want to know, but because I was afraid to hear what the answer would be.

"Mother, who gave birth to me?"

"What?"

"Mother, I know you don't have a womb. So who was the woman who carried me for nine months?"

Her mouth fell open but no words came out. She finally said, "Why does it matter?"

"I just want to know who she was. Is it someone I know?"

Tears dripped down her face. "Am I not good enough for you? Well, of course I'm not—I'm white and queer!"

"Mother, that's not true. I love you more than anyone in this world! You're the only family I have now."

"She was a prostitute!" my mother blurted out. "Some little citified Oluchi girl who was begging and selling herself in DakCrete. Stevedore paid for the use of her womb. We kept her here at the clinic. You were taken away from her at birth, so she never knew you. She contracted AIDS and died when you were about six."

"What was her name?"

"Zess Epiphany."

"Zess," I repeated, *"delicate one."*

Later, as we sat on my mother's bed and listened to her Fleetwood Mac albums, she pulled out a red leather box that I'd never seen before. A lock adorned the front of it. "I've waited years to share these photographs with you."

As my mother unlocked the box and rifled through the photos, a pamphlet slipped out and dropped to the floor. While she arranged the pictures, I bent over the bed to reach down and grab the pamphlet's worn, yellowed pages. Above a caption that read *Ajowaland, 1651* was a drawing of a voluptuous, naked, sex-crazed African woman, her face in ecstasy as a group of slave-trading white men groped and fondled her. On the opposite page was an image of a tall, honorable-looking white missionary, his hands outstretched as he preached to white settlers and a naked tribe of black savages. This caption read: *The white woman is the virtuous part of the Bible; her hand is fair. But the black woman is the sex in the Bible; everything about her is wicked.*

"Here they are," Mother said, removing a rubber band from around a thin stack of photos. I quickly tucked the pamphlet into my pocket. "If you never understood anything in this world that I told you before, I want you to understand this: Stevedore was not a homosexual, Eternity. We were simply of a scientific mind."

Then she began showing me the photographs—two little boys, around ten or eleven, standing proudly next to a lemonade stand; then the same two boys, now in their teens, smiling as they waxed a gorgeous classic Chevy.

"We grew up with each other," Dr. Juliet continued, "two all-American boys who went to high school and college together and wanted to be astronauts and brain surgeons and chemists. Here, look at this."

It was a photograph that had their names written at the bottom in blue ink: *Stevedore Frankenheimer and Julian Howell. Cleveland All-City Basketball Finals, 1964.*

"We were best friends, your father and I, closer than brothers. We did everything together, except have sex— we never had sex while I was a guy. No. But, of course, rarely did we run into women who thought how we thought or were obsessed with molecules and biology and physics like we were. And then there was the little secret that I had kept from Stevedore all our lives—the fact that I was in love with him. It nearly killed him when I told him I was breaking off our friendship and going away to Finland to do lab research. He couldn't understand why I didn't want to be friends anymore—so I told him the truth. That I was in love with him and that I knew, from all the girls he'd been fucking since we were like fourteen, that he wasn't the least bit gay. And so I left for Helsinki, and then a few months later Stevedore wrote to me . . . asking if I would allow him to transform me into a female so that we could be together. For us, being two scientists, it was just practical problem solving. X equals Y."

Dr. Juliet smiled and caressed my cheek with the soft knuckles of her large bony hand. Her gaze was epic coolness.

"Your acceptance of me," she went on, "means everything to me, Eternity. Like so many scientists, your father and I came to Africa expecting to make a difference. We wanted to use our brilliance to save the world by growing hearts, lungs, and kidneys for people who needed transplants. But somehow, once you start playing behind the steering wheel of God, you realize just how powerful it is to be the imagination driving the natural world. You tap into this willful, compassionate, insane force of wonder and, well, now I fear that too many Gods can only make the world worse off. I don't think we've helped anything."

I lied and said, "Well, you helped me, Mother."

For a moment I hugged her close. Then she pulled back from me and said, "There's another picture I have to show you. A picture of your birth mother, Zess Epiphany."

I grabbed it from her hands and stared at it, crying with the most conflicted agony and joy.

"She was so pretty." I studied the young, vivacious, chocolate-skinned Oluchi girl in the photo. But whereas Orisha and I were identical in every way, Zess Epiphany looked nothing like me whatsoever. She had simply been a human incubator; Orisha's genetic material is what I am.

"Zess was like you," promised Dr. Juliet. "She loved to swim."

M MAGAZINE QUESTION #33

Yes, I love to swim—to swim away from shadows.

And later that night I lay awake in bed, not only swimming in tears for the arms that feel so empty without Hope, and not only revisiting the details of all my mother's hard-won revelations that day, but also haunted by the words that the missionary John Theodosius van Elker had written in 1651 on the pamphlet pages that I'd stolen and read over and over:

> But the black woman is the sex in the Bible; everything about her is wicked. It would be better, I say, if you gallant traders and brethren of the civilized world took some shame in what you do at night. I promise to flog the very next shiphand that comes to me, not even grown yet, professing some love for the black man's mother and requesting that I marry them—using this Bible. For shame, I say, for shame! To be adjourned with these Jezebel lepers of the wild—these tar pagan sinners who openly flaunt their naked lust and whore-mongering and have not produced a single son that was the white man's equal in either deed, intellect, or heart.

I say to you that Africa is a wasteland of the most back-ward immorality inhabited by the cursed children of Ham, and surely the Lord sent us to save her—but we cannot save her by compromising the trinity of our own purity, and we cannot rule the black man through the black man's mother. Everything she touches is defiled by her darkness.

Let us pray that Africa repents. Let us pray for her salvation.

Even in a strange land, away from our white mothers, I say—we must uphold the honor of the white woman! For she is the virtue in the Bible, the prize above rubies, the jewel of God's heart; her hand is fair! Those white traders and seafarers in disagreement—and I see your shameful faces throughout the crowd—you shant continue these romances with whores! We cannot rule the black world through the black man's mother, and the black man cannot rule the white world through the white man's mother—and so we must never lose sight of which mother goes on top. Our very survival depends on it, that we not give in to temptation . . . and be asunder, the utter darkness of Africa's damnation.

A few weeks later, when my mother and I went to Dak-Crete to watch *The Racist* at the cinema, it was all suddenly clear, the brilliant scheme in van Elker's fearful sermon. For on the movie screen, larger than life itself, my whole being had lost all representation—the beautiful African mulatto actress, whose egg-and-milk complexion and flowing hair and tenuous upper-class voice sounding and looking nothing whatsoever like me, became a symbolic image of van Elker's truth—*white men cannot rule the black world through the black man's mother.* And so on the screen, while the impassioned African mulatto actress derided the black street youths for bleaching their skin and literally knocked the whitening pills out of their hands just as I had done in a previous life, it was still the image of the white man's mother that she represented. It was still the voice of some American writer emanating from her throat in poor imitation of mines; it was still her flowing hair swinging like the lynch rope and the rape tassel; it was still the light face and European features of white rule and white comfort—so fearful of black power that they could not depict my black body as human wholeness. I was too black to represent myself, too pure for them to ever dominate—so they lightened me. And even with the good intentions of this African mulatto actress, it was still the erasure of me and my people from our own landscape that her image represented, the removal of black humans from their own bodies. There in the dark, watching this American watering-down of my beauty, I stared at the blue sheen in my charcoal hands and arms—and came to understand that I was the sexy part of the bible. The thing that God so despised. Just as tenaciously as I had accepted that I was a clone and possessed no soul. I embraced it. I welcomed it. I wrapped myself up in it.

The sexy part of the Bible.

Thou wicked, sinful leper of utter blackness and mother of the black man. Yes, I determined, I will stand black as all black put together. I am Eternity; I am the sexy part of the Bible.

M MAGAZINE: LONDON, NEW YORK, PARIS
A foo-foo . . . I thought choo knew

AND TURN!!

The paparazzi click-clicked our every move, and during outfit changes backstage, rumors abounded that Brad Pitt and Angelina Jolie were watching from the side flank and that director Spike Lee had been spotted in the audience along with pop queen Mariah Carey. But for those of us up on the catwalk, there was no time to spy who was there in the dark—and besides, the only person out there who I cared to impress was my handsome new boyfriend, James Lord.

A foo-foo . . . I thought choo knew

AND TURN!!

Naomi Campbell, the best in the business now that Iman had retired, locked her hips and pivoted flawlessly, her panther-perfect torso imploding the open mouths of all onlookers with a stunned silence, their very souls entranced as she drifted like some goddess they had dreamt into being back down the runway—then it was Linda floating along like some great blond fantasy apparition; and then Amber, gorgeous and elegant as living, breathing silk; and then stunning Alek as the Queen of Sheba; and then Kate giving us 1930s Katherine Hepburn; and Ling-Nara the Swan demonstrating how tall Asians can be; and then the goddess of all goddesses, Claudia herself; and then . . .

A foo-foo . . . I thought choo knew

AND TURN!!

I was out there! My fifty-inch legs moving as though they had come into Paris with an agenda all their own, *thank God*—my legs were working it. Hands on hips, mouth puckered aristocratically, and my little Negroid caboose adding a touch of "woman-got-damn" to my six-foot starving-African figure, I felt as though I were some glorious meteor crashing to earth while two white girls in front kept screaming out my name: "Eternity . . . you're the bomb! Go, Eternity!"

I stopped in the middle of the runway, the popping flashbulbs catching in my glass slippers like champagne froth as I pivoted with an exasperated underaged sexiness and expertly held a glamour pose mere seconds enough for the paparazzi to click-click the flowing white silk and lace Dane Goddard evening robe I was modeling. Then, as quickly as my outer space–colored body had become the center of the universe, I undid the belt, unleashing my shapely charcoal legs, and sashayed back down the catwalk, my onion-booty swinging like a pendulum and my mannequin-perfect face never once betraying that elitist expression that goes so well with decadence: *I'm the shit, and I know it.*

But backstage, when I broke into a triumphant smile and exhaled as though my joy had been bottled up for centuries, a fan suddenly came running up to me, his voice praising me excitedly as his arms stretched out in my direction. His white hands gripped a chocolate-colored, child-sized plastic doll, its glassy marble eyes and smiling goo-goo mouth boring into me as though it might tell.

Caught by surprise, I screamed in horror, my knees giving way as I fell into my own hollering, my heart and veins trembling beneath the skin, and I peed on myself.

"Eternity!?" the other models and stylists called out in concern.

"What the hell is wrong with her?"

"Is she on drugs?"

I bent to the floor, hyperventilating and attempting to keep my eyes to the carpet so that I wouldn't have to see the doll again, but the fan was trying to help me up, and the doll's cold plastic legs and hands kept poking into me until I thought surely I'd have a heart attack.

I heard James Lord, my handsome Brit, coming to my rescue. He shoved people out of the way and yelled, "Get that away from her—she's got a phobia about dolls!"

Then the doll dropped on the floor, its glassy, curly lashed eyes locking directly into mines. I passed out.

RIGHT NOW, 2004

Rector Sniff, the reporter from M magazine, is asking if I'm aware that "sexy superstar rapper" King Sea Horse Twee is staying in the same resort that I am. When I gently nod that yes, I'm aware of it, Sniff's mouth waters as he points out that Sea Horse and I are two of the sexiest celebrities from the African continent right now, and what a frenzy of publicity it would ignite if the world thought we were *circling* one another.

As he fishes in my eyes for something to nibble on, I freeze all memory of my night swim the other evening when Sea Horse had come up behind me in the dark waters, his black fists pouncing against the nose and gills of the baby shark that had innocently waded into the shallows and was just about to sideswipe me. That was how we finally met—his muscular naked arms clamping onto my topless upper torso and guiding me back to shore despite my haughty protests about being adept at igun, the art of flipping a shark over on its back, which completely paralyzes it, in or out of water.

Yes, I freeze the image of Sea Horse and me standing on the warm starry beach, his eyes on my flesh as
I toweled down my bare breasts and flat-as-a-flounder
stomach—his ashen chocolate lips shaped like a butter-
fly pursing with a hunger to kiss. I arrest all memory of
the feeling that I had left one shark in the sea only to
come to land with the king of the species. I obliterate
the touch of his fingers caressing my face as he gushed
in wonder, "You are so . . . *black*." I disassemble the penetrating fascination in Sea Horse's words: "I thought
you were a mannequin or a doll that they painted up
like this in magazines or generated with a computer. I
thought, no woman is that beautiful, that celestial, but
in dreams."

"And of course you're a liar," I had laughed. "Don't
fuck with me, rap boy—I've killed men!"

Which had caused Sea Horse to laugh back at me,
proclaiming, "You can't be a killer. You've got the face of
a nurse, the most spiritual eyes I've ever seen, and your
voice is tender like the lonely hearted."

"And *you* have a wife!"

"I'm a true African, I have three wives."

And though this encounter took place against an African sky, our brief enchantment symbolized the new
world's greatest taboo—the hand of a very black man
caressing the face of the blackest woman, with no shred
of light entering into it, utter darkness alone representing God.

Having noticed all my life that watching me from
the rear as I depart is some kind of instinctual treat for
black men, I slowly walked away without looking back
as his voice became a distant echo. And then it bothered

me: *I've never been with a black man!* I made up my mind that very moment that Sea Horse would be the first—just once for sex, just once before I left paradise and returned to James Lord's abbey in England. A hit-and-run.

Rector Sniff: "Well, surely you two have met?"

At my dressing table, where the candlelight can fool you into thinking I'm a doll or a lifelike puppet, I lie convincingly. As a matter of fact, my whole interview with M magazine has been a lie. Nothing that I'm telling *you* have I shared with anyone else on earth, and especially not with Sniff. So I lie, "I've seen him a few times on the beach, talking and being affectionate with his wife. But no, I've never met him. I really know very little about him, other than that he's famous."

"He's becoming a political powder keg in this country. He makes the government nervous. What are your views about West Cassavaland's upcoming elections?"

I smile girlishly, pretending that I'm not only dumb but *embarrassed* to be dumb. I say, "I'm not much for politics, sorry."

"What about the nude photo sessions you did for *Sports Illuminated*—many people complain that you're perpetuating the stereotype of the backward naked African woman."

It is my response to this question that literally doubles my fame around the globe overnight. But I don't know this when I answer, "I don't see the covering of women's breasts as clean or decent. I see it the opposite. I am not a Christian; I am not Islamic. I am not ashamed of my ancestors' nudity. I learned from the Oluchi women that to be naked outdoors is to be closest to God; the cleanest and most decent a woman can be. I guess you could call me . . . the sexy part of the Bible. Though I live in England, shop in Paris, and party in New York, I'll always be that raisin-headed little girl chopping cassava and stirring the clay pots."

Rector raises his eyebrow ever so. "Tell our readers what brought you to modeling and to England."

JAMES

I could feel the vibration of what was going on. Already overcome with anger and feelings of betrayal, I turned the latch and opened the door to find Dr. Juliet cooing and writhing on her bed as she was being fucked by our scientist from India, Dr. Gobi Kadir. Something in me wanted to scream out, *Get off my mommy!* or, *She belongs to my father!* But her pale white chicken legs were spread wide open and his tanned skinny body humped between them feverishly, the hairy dark gingerbread of his balls flopping against my mother's vagina as though the nut sack and pussy were laughing at me.

"Ouuuhhhhh, Gobi, *fuck me! Fuck me!*"

"Take it all, Dr. Frankenheimer, take it all!"

In my whole life, I'd scarcely noticed the blue fingerprint-like shadows beneath my mother's tired eyes or the crow's feet and wrinkles around her mouth, until one afternoon, after emerging from being chased around the bed by Dr. Kadir, grinning and laughing and looking silly, which just annoyed me so much, the wrinkles and tiredness miraculously vanished. Attention from a man made her limber and giddy; made her someone I didn't know.

"Mother, everyone in the clinic is gossiping about you."

"That's none of my business, Eternity."

Hope had been dead about three months by then and, with not a clue about what to do with my life, I had given in to my mother's wish that I attend the University of DakCrete. Out of the blue, she began to exhibit the most embarrassingly unprofessional behavior—for instance, insisting that the whole clinic staff eat dinner together nightly while she sits on Dr. Kadir's lap at the head of the table, her laughing face completely oblivious to the disapproving glare of Dr. Quicken.

"I can't take seeing you with men other than Stevedore," I told her in private.

"You won't have to. You'll be at school in DakCrete."

Even though I wasn't yet aware of my mother's new cloning project, I knew there were things about my mother that I didn't want to find out. I realized that I needed to do more than go to university—I needed to leave the nest for good. But, of course, it was the *way* that I left the nest that surprised me.

For weeks, Dr. Juliet had opened the clinic as a sort of bed and breakfast for her rich friends from places like MIT, London, Brussels, Copenhagen, Sag Harbor, and the Soviet Union. Most of them were nice boring scientists, writers, and socialites. But on one occasion, as I walked into the drawing room, there stood the most stunningly gorgeous older white guy, dressed up like some kind of Indiana Jones–type adventurer. His hands were on his hips and the first thing I noticed was that he had arms like Popeye the Sailor—huge and ham-shaped with thick blond hair. I was attracted to him immediately.

"Eternity, I want you to meet someone that your father greatly admired—this is Dr. James Lord of Marble Arch, London. You've seen his name in my science journals throughout the years. He's a cryptozoologist."

"A what?"

"A cryptozoologist," James reiterated in a voice so deep it went straight to my bones and warmed the small of my back. "A person who searches for cryptids."

"Cryptids?"

He kissed my hand as a greeting. But the way his sky-blue eyes pressed against my flesh, I felt like he was *eating* me. I could see right away that like many Caucasian people who travel to Africa, he had an intense fascination with those of us whose skin is actually coal-black and silvery. He had a look that said, *I cannot believe there are humans this black.*

"Yes, cryptids. Rumored or mythological animals that are presumed to exist."

"Oooh!" I gasped, suddenly realizing who he was. "You're that man who led all those expeditions looking for the Loch Ness monster."

"Affirmative," he grinned proudly. "My late father was actually a part of the team that was able to prove that cryptids exist. The whole scientific world was under the impression that the coelacanth fish had been extinct for more than sixty million years and that only their fossils still existed—but in 1938, my father's expedition caught living, breathing coelacanths off the coast of Madagascar. Right now," he carried on, "I have my eye on a much bigger quarry. I'm planning an expedition for 2005 and 2006 to hunt down Africa's legendary Mokele-Mbembe."

Now *that* caught my attention, because even though

the entire world has heard of the Loch Ness monster and America's Big Foot—very few outside Africa have heard anything about the Congo's half-elephant, half-dragon swamp dinosaur, Mokele-Mbembe (Stopper of Rivers). The creature is sometimes reported to come ashore and eat only plants and trees before vanishing beneath the superdeep waters of Likouala Lakes. But other times it has been said to kill villagers who try to catch it, or to turn over the boats of the great white hunters who have come for more than a century now to try to prove the thing exists.

"Pray you don't get eaten," I said, seriously.

"Oh, I'm a firm believer in prayer." That startled me, because he was the first white person or scientist I'd ever met who believed in God while standing *outside* the church.

Later, I learned that my mother was paying Dr. Lord ten thousand dollars to build her a yamba garden behind the clinic. In West Cassavaland, the people refer to the highest quality marijuana as "yamba"—and although I knew that small fact, what I had never known and what James taught me is that plants, trees, and vegetables contain sperm and egg, and that they mate in the earth to create seeds, and that they come in sexes—male, female, or something called "perfect flower," which means bisexual, or rather that the plant in question, an avocado for instance, has both sperm and egg to reproduce itself without a mate.

I found it fascinating and James Lord and I became like buddies, going out before sunlight and raking the soil before we leaked milk-tea, livestock urine, and gunpowder that the local police had donated for our project into the ground using some liposuction cannulas that we got from Dr. Juliet's selector precision box.

"You always make a batch of sinsemilla."

"Ha?"

"Here," James said, handing me a magnifying glass. "It's your job to detect all male marijuana. The males don't have any white or pink hairs—just fat little balls on a stick. In our sinsemilla crop, you remove all males on sight. They mustn't pollinate the females if we're to cultivate reefer with a superior kick. The Indian doctor wants it strong."

We built a dirge with netting to separate the full-sun weed crop from the shade weed crop, and James Lord kept me in stitches with hilarious stories—such as the time he witnessed tennis star Venus Williams win her first Wimbledon trophy and how annoyed England's royal family became when her father, Richard Williams, jumped on center court yelling, "Straight outta Compton!"

"You remind me of my father," I told him one afternoon as we were frying bananas, coconut, and pineapple for lunch.

"Dr. Juliet had a little talk with me this morning. She's concerned that I might take advantage of you. She got carried away and made some threats."

Avoiding eye contact, I said, "My mother has nothing to worry about—you treat me like a son."

"Apparently, the whole clinic is gossiping about us."

"Well, that's none of our business."

"Do you like me treating you as a son?"

Stirring the pan, I looked over and pierced his blue-eyed gaze with the most sinfully seductive biblical stare I could muster. How dare he try to dare me.

"I hear you had a child that just died," he said.

"Yes."

"You barely look like more than a child yourself."

"I've never been a child, James—*ever*."

He examined me for a moment, intrigued. "Where's your baby's father?"

"He's dead."

"AIDS?"

"Oh, no. Nothing like that. I'm clean and my baby was clean. The father was, uh, hiking through the jungle and got eaten by red ants. We don't like to talk about it."

"So what do you do, Eternity? Are you going to be a scientist like your parents?"

"No, I hate too much thinking."

"You know, Eternity, I can't help wondering why a girl as beautiful and enigmatic as you doesn't have a bounty of young men coming to call on her. There's this mystery about you. It's quite alluring."

Enigmatic? What did that mean?

I reminded him, "I've been raised, touched, and handled by white people, James—English is the only language I speak fluently. The Africans consider me worse than a Been-to. They don't trust me. Even though plenty of their sons have tried to fuck me, they would never seriously consider marrying a girl like me. I'm a weirdo, and now that everyone wants to look like the Pogo Metis Signare, the mulatto upper class, I'm too black."

"I love your color," he said dreamily. "It's so erotic to me, because it's unbelievable. You're literally panther-black. I've never made love to a woman . . . that black."

I laughed. "Tell me, Dr. Lord. Adventuring through Africa as you do—how many black women *have* you fucked?"

"Oh, lots," he said. "Mostly the ones in England, though. I like African women, West Indian women, Asians, white women, of course, Spanish women, fat women."

"Fat women?"

"Fat women give the best blowjobs, because they're always hungry."

I laughed again and shook my head. "I don't know about you, James. It seems you've been with an awful lot of women."

"I don't have a bint right now." It was apparently hip in London to use the Arabic word when identifying one's girlfriend. "And England's a dreary place without a nice bint, a sweet lass. So tell me this, Eternity: would you be open to an older man courting you the old-fashioned way?"

"What do you mean?"

"I want something from you, but I don't know what it is yet. Well, other than that *thing* between males and females. But I can't very well get it here in Africa with your mother on my tail. What if I treat you to a vacation in London? No sex, no pressure—just dinners out, long walks, and sightseeing. I suspect you like to dance and go shopping?"

I was flabbergasted but definitely open to the invitation. "And where would I stay, James?"

"I have a large house with numerous guest rooms. But if you'd prefer your own hotel suite, it's up to you."

* * *

I truly hated London at first. Because I wanted to be James's girlfriend, however, I stayed well beyond the initial seven-day vacation. In fact, I soon moved into his house in the snooty, rich neighborhood of Great Cumberland by Marble Arch. Nobody looked at me funny for being there (mainly because James hired a white uniformed maid named Sarah to escort me around), but I felt isolated. All around me were these lily-white and imitation lily-white biracial rich girls who spent whole conversations comparing the ringtones on their mobile phones, or praising me, the newcomer, for being "so fucking gorgeous to be so fucking burnt." They all dressed in what they called "peasant chic," but, of course, because I know peasants and how they actually dress, I just found it pretentious. I couldn't help but become a snob languishing behind the walls of James's abbey, and before long they nicknamed me Garbo.

James fucked me for the first time on the night I moved into his place, just a few hours after we'd shared a candlelit dinner. Five nights later it became lovemaking. Sweetly measured tenderness with the most ferociously masculine stroke, wading into the hot pink flesh that lay just beneath my coal-black pussy lips; and, in fact, because my pussy's so black, he liked looking at it for long spells before he'd just tear into it with his mouth and tongue—eating it like crazy.

"You said this was only a vacation!" my mother screamed by phone from Africa.

"But Mother, I'm his woman now."

"James Lord is a rogue serial-fucker, Eternity! He doesn't have one woman!"

I tried not to believe her at first, but then came all

the signs, the first one being his stern admonition, "If you get pregnant, love . . . I'll kick you out and never speak to you again. I don't want to be box-tricked by anybody's snot-nosed brats." And then after that, it bothered me that we never drove out to the country to meet his parents. Additionally, his work as a cryptozo-ologist took him on adventures all over the world: Nepal one minute, Hiroshima the next. The Black Sea, Mexico, Siberia, and his preparations to hunt down our lake monster in Africa.

"You're always gone," I complained one morning af-ter he'd made the most ravenous love to me.

"I can't stop until I find it."

"Find what?"

"I don't know, but it's out there. Something the world has never seen. In a lake or a cavern beneath the earth, in the jungles, under the frozen ice—I don't know where it is, but I won't feel like a real man until I've found it and captured it."

We did have a golden period where we held hands everywhere we went, working out together at the gym over by Ally Pally and going to see popular local bands like the Others, Bolt-Thrower, and Bathory. But he soon started what my mother calls "spotting" (sneaking oc-casional extra pussy from hit-and-runs with anonymous women). Then one week—when I had been led to be-lieve he was on assignment in Greenland looking for an ancient bearded prune lizard—his glassy-eyed party grin suddenly turned up in every London gossip sheet from the *Mirror* to the *Sun*, his arms draped around a thirty-something blond, pointy-nosed *East of the End* soap actress.

The caption not only said that they were dating, but for the first time I became aware of James's son, Ian. According to the newspaper, Ian lived in Australia with his mother, retired model Christy Twelvetrees, who the paper referred to as the love of James's life. Truly, it was a blow for me. When I went out to get air and weep beneath clouds, which is where I thought God (who I didn't believe in) would surely give me some idea of what to do, I realized that everyone in Marble Arch had seen the gossip rags. More than that, they were thrilled that such a rich, gorgeous white catch as James Lord was apparently dumping his African novelty piece for a more appropriate dime!

I called James, of course, demanding to know what was going on and why he didn't tell me about Ian, but all he did was make fun of my hysteria. He said that I should stop reading the newspapers, make myself busy around the house, and start looking for some piece of jewelry that I'd like him to get me. Not an engagement ring, mind you, but some bauble. He said, "I love you, Eternity. You're in my house because you're the one I want to come home to."

And like any other stupid girl in love, desperate to hold on to I-don't-know-what, I tried to make do with that—until the doorbell rang one afternoon with an unexpected surprise.

Sarah answered the door and dutifully announced, "There's a Miss Juliet Frankenheimer to see you, madame."

My jaw dropped open in disbelief as my mother swept in like the Queen of England—or worse, America's Hillary Clinton. Her shoulders were tense like a hawk as she clutched in her hand one of the gossip rags with photos of James Lord and his soap actress.

"Mother, you came all the way to London!"

"Yes, Eternity, we need to have a little chat—about white men and black men."

Over roast beef and Yorkshire pudding, I noticed that my mother was now a full-fledged pothead, her watery blue eyes calm and pinkish after I'd given her permission to light up, her tongue and fingers rolling up a marijuana cigarette like an expert, lighting, sucking, and exhaling as though it were second nature. She offered me a hit, and after I declined, she began to speak in the same clinical science-lady logic that I'd grown up with.

"The white man and the black man are both men, and, of course, men like as much variety in life as they can get. But there's a major distinction, Eternity: the white man is the lord and ruler of this world, and the black man has no power. There isn't a black ruler on earth who can make a political decision, internationally, without the permission of white men. Be it Europe or America, somewhere he has to answer to white men. So it should be obvious that the white man has something of value to protect—and that is his *whiteness*. Do you understand what I'm saying?"

I didn't yet, but I nodded anyway.

Dr. Juliet took a deep breath and went on, painful as it was. "Eternity, a black man has nothing of value to protect, especially not his physical blackness, because his race and color are seen as inferior—therefore, he rarely faces any objections to marrying and procreating with a woman who isn't black, because if anything, the world sees the lightening of his progeny as an improvement over his darkness—a gain in status. Do you still follow?"

I nodded, growing angry.

"A white man has to protect his whiteness, because his whiteness is the most valuable thing in this world, and he can only be born from or procreated by a white woman. No others."

A tear ran down my cheek.

"I want you to remain with James, if that's what you want. But as your mother, it's also my responsibility to make sure you realize exactly just what cards are in the deck. As a black girl—especially a girl as pure black as you are—there is the awful likelihood that his interest in you might only go so far, that it might have a ceiling. No matter how much he adores you . . ."

I bowed my head, unable to hear the rest of her words. It was and is the truth—that the eyes of the world do not consider me to be a good mate for any man.

I am not the one who the world revolves around.

OPEN CEILING

Hope had died and I had no soul.

That was a big part of the reason I stayed with James. But also because he reminded me so much of Stevedore, spoiling and doting on me. Naturally, people believed that I put up with James's indiscretions because he was a white man first and a rich man second. It wasn't true, but what else could they think?

I shivered with tears of gratitude whenever he returned to his lair and made love to me. Our best conversations always came after sex. I learned to cook, learned to play his favorite game, chess, learned as much as I could about the history of cryptozoology, kept myself as beautiful as I possibly could, and then one day, in all my bored loneliness, I accidentally changed my entire life by deciding to board the tube at Oxford Street. A famous German photographer was on the train that day and it's as simple as that—he saw me.

"You look like a mannequin!" the photographer blurted out in amazement as I searched for an open seat. "A doll, wound up and walking around like a human!"

His aggression startled me, and I halted in insectlike repose.

"Mother got-damn, hold that pose!" he screamed, pulling out his camera. "You look like an alien! Don't move."

Within a matter of weeks I was on a billboard at Piccadilly. They had a photo of me in the *Mirror* with the caption: *Famed photographer presents his latest creation—Eternity.*

It happened so fast. Like connective tissue coming together.

The photographer—whom I immediately realized was gay and therefore okay to run around with—took me to the BBC studios where he personally directed me in a television commercial for Second Moon Cosmetics. Tall, wire-skinny, and white as chalk, with a dramatically black Louise Brooks–like bob that he constantly had to flick out of his blue eyes, the photographer tortured me by making me say this one line over and over again: "It's me . . . Eternity . . . accept no imitations."

"Goddamnit, bitch, you sound like you're reciting the multiplication tables! Say it again—with passion!"

"It's me . . . Eternity . . . accept no imitations."

"No, no, NO!"

"It's *me* . . . *Eternity* . . . accept no imitations."

"Can someone put on a Diana Ross tune? Something larger than the sun and glamorexic? Quiet on the set!"

"It's me . . . Eternity . . . accept no imitations."

"Goddamnit, bitch. What's your boyfriend's name again?"

"James . . ."

"Pretend you're in the doorway of your bedroom—catching James in bed with some sexy Japanese chick. And he's got exactly three seconds to make a decision as to which one of you he wants to spend the rest of—"

"*It's me!* . . . *ETERNITY* . . ." I nearly cried. "*Accept NO imitations.*"

"There you go! And cut . . . and print!"

The studio crew applauded.

James was in Hiroshima searching for ancient bearded lizards. He didn't know a thing about what I was doing. By the time he returned to London, I'd been magically transformed into the fashion world's most sought-after model, a trio of gay men teaching me everything—how to walk, how to put on makeup, how to pose without looking like I'm posing. After they were finished, I did my first catwalk in Paris, flew in and out of Milan's Baccarat show, and shot a photo spread for *Miss Priss* magazine against the Moroccan desert.

James came home exhausted and frustrated from not finding his bearded prune lizard. During those first few hours, as we lay on the bed watching television, me giving him a blowjob, on came the most startlingly beautiful charcoal woman, luxuriating in the pond of a tropical garden—and James mumbled, "I know her from somewhere."

The music blared as the camera panned in for the close-up. The figure arrogantly declared, *"It's me . . . Eternity . . . Accept NO imitations."*

James jumped up. "Hey, what the—"

I started giggling as the voiceover announced: *"Earth's Eternity, the new mud moisturizer for younger-looking skin."*

James nibbled on my ear, whisper-laughing that I was gorgeous, and kissed and poked up inside me until that whole night stretched out like some dreamy magic carpet ride.

We even went horseback riding the next morning. But when we returned home for lunch there was some woman calling, giggling on the answering machine about how much fun she had with James in Japan, and that she loved her necklace and looked forward to seeing him in Australia. It was like he wanted me to know about his cheating.

Later that night, as we dined at the Savoy Steakhouse, he took my hand and slipped a very modest diamond engagement ring on it. "I want us to get married, Eternity. But before that takes place, I need to get the humping wolf out of my system. I need two good years to just fuck around—and then I'm all yours."

I didn't say anything about the ring on my finger. I simply looked down into my steak, the pinkish meat juicy with blood.

"Will you wait to be my wife?"

Out of desperation I nodded affirmatively.

The next morning I talked on the phone to my mother, who charged right in: "You're not being very scientific about this. Have you even met his parents yet?" There was a long, dead silence before she continued. "Well, have you? Eternity, James is not going to marry you. You're just another rare cryptid to him. You're a hostage in his home and he enjoys fucking you and wants you to put up with his global spotting. And even if he did marry you, once you let a man cheat, he'll always cheat. I'll bet that Japanese bitch has an engagement ring bigger than yours. I know men, Eternity—I used to be one!"

"That's your marijuana talking, Dr. Juliet."

"So what if it is? Grass brings the truth out. And you know what else? This is what you get for fucking your father all those years. Stevedore was *my* husband and I had to look the other way—"

"You and Stevedore raised me to do that! I didn't ask for it!" I slammed the phone down.

Two days later, a slew of pale fashion people had me perched on an antique chair, all dressed up in a satin ball gown with Jell-O-red, Russian sapphire rubies fastened around my collarbone, as they shot a layout for Symphony perfume. I suddenly caught a glimpse of myself in the mirror that beckoned from across the way. I saw how to someone like James I might be a cryptid, no less exotic and mysterious than a bearded prune lizard or the Loch Ness monster.

Modeling is a jittery, jumping affair. It requires you to be vicarious, to perfect a certain brand of fakeness. Good with evoking the naïve coat hanger, I was sent for shoots in Milan, Copenhagen, Barcelona, and Paris. It was in Paris that James caught up with me. At Club Djoon X, we danced to Snake Girl's techno smash "I've

Never Been with a Black Man Before," then fucked like bunnies in my hotel room.

The next morning, when James was sitting up in bed so that I could feed him like a baby, he finally blurted out what he'd come all the way to Paris to say: "I had a very strange dream about us."

I stopped feeding him, but I remained silent.

"You were pregnant with my child, and I was happy about it."

"Don't worry, I'm on the pill."

"Then maybe you should get off it."

We stared at each other for a very long moment. Then I said, "Yeah, I can just see myself strutting down the runway with a stomach out to here, posing and pivoting. I'm one of the few black models getting steady work, and I'm new—I have to *fight* to secure my career."

"So tell me, my future wife, what's next after Paris?"

"Home," I said, "to Africa. There's a journalist from M magazine coming to do a feature article about me, and then I'm taking two weeks to do nothing but rest at a resort. Visit my mother."

"Sometimes I wonder what your real story is."

"I'm a woman, James. That's always my story."

I'VE NEVER BEEN WITH A BLACK MAN BEFORE

On some nights the moon in Africa can burn down on a person's shoulders with all the intensity of the sun. And tonight, at last, I'm going to dare to do what I thought I'd never do—cheat on James Lord. Sea Horse and I both know that I'm going to let him fuck me out in the coastal shadows where it's dark and rocky. He knows this because we've been running into each other at the shore-line for a few nights now, saying little things back and forth, our black bodies glistening like dolphin hides as we spear ourselves beneath a periwinkle moon.

"You're an Ajowan," Sea Horse had teased a few nights ago. "Do you still pray to the ocean?"

I told him that I was raised by whites and Oluchi people, and therefore didn't know much about the Ajo-wan clan. But I did remember Nana Oluchi taking me for long walks on the beach. She'd kneel beside me and say, "The Ajowans believe that the ocean is a black woman—the Goddess Ajowa. The Ajowans believe that they came from the sea, and that in ancient times their tribe could live underwater for days at a time. You, Eternity, are an Ajowan."

I sure believe it now as I take to the water, my body entering the rolling see-through lavender of both sky and moon, the heat of the night caressing my flesh no matter how deep I go. Then I hear King Sea Horse Twee calling to me from the dunes—"Eyyy, mermaid, wait!"—and look back to see his tall, naked chocolate body diving in.

I hear his voice again from the other night: *Do you still pray to the ocean?* The decimal of chambers had formed the cadence in his coca-boy accent as though he'd been praying when he asked it. Oddly enough, I crave prayer, ritual, and religion—the naked ocean sex like moments in a baptized fever; the illicit ecstasy and sinfulness of cheating, kissing, caressing, licking, and fucking—saltier than the waves in a wet dream. I want it so bad—to ex-perience a black man's penis up inside me, deeper than my cervix. Yet the butterflies in my stomach threaten to weigh me down to the moon spots on the sea floor, and as I contain all that rage and soul, cooking like molasses in the folds of my pussy's sweetest ever cat-wishing, I plunge beneath the warm depths, my imagination descending as well into a kind of chant-prayer. My body is swimming as far out as it can—to escape him and get beyond the coral reef garden, beyond the clear waters—to the dark, murky deep ocean where sharks are known to patrol at night searching for baby tuna or dolphins to bite, rape, and drown.

And just as I fear that I might be going too far out, I glance up and see the purple robes of sky flowing like ribbons into my eyes, into the sea, and into all the edges of the world. I notice the white light from every prayer that is being prayed around the world twinkling within those robes. There, in the starry ocean-sky, I get goosebumps, some intuitive part of me touched at the nerve endings by what I can only describe as spirits (feelings), ancestors (hunches), the salted breeze watching over me, the realization that though I was lost in the animalistic preamble of the wilderness lust—both inside me and in the wilderness—it suddenly seems that the ocean indeed *is* a woman, her sloshing black face and her sparkling dips and swirls activating some primitive knowing intensity within me. It is ever-mysterious and holy, holding and handling me like a mother rocks her child, the beat of my heart slowing from a pulsating heat to a near-deadly stillness. Right then—at the point of stillness, my body going unconscious, the skeleton of my silhouette sinking fast into the satiny black waters surely to drown—Sea Horse torpedoes up, snatching me from hypnosis, and rocks me back into wakefulness. It's a manly moment.

My eyes blink, my flesh and bones reignited by the warmth of his own, his sheer power breaking the surface of the sea as he handles me roughly, completely unaware of the telepathic chill I've just experienced. He presses his body against mines, the rock-hardness of his penis forceful against my leg as his mouth struggles, hungrily, to find and get control of mines. And although he's just saved my life, I don't understand why one of his hands is groping at my breasts.

"Stop it," I say, unexpectedly.

But he doesn't stop—so I slap the shit out of him.

"I said get the fuck off me!"

"You play games! Every night you're a different woman. Where's the one who wanted me to fuck her?"

Suddenly cold and awkwardly ashamed of myself for having teased him the last few nights, I turn and swim away toward one of the small coastal slave islands where in the daytime Ajowan children congregate to feed the birds and dolphins that frequent the lagoon.

I emerge from the ocean as though leaving a womb to perch against the rocks. I lean back against the solid boulders, oblivious to the lizards and insects that live within them. My skin imitates the surface of the night sea, shimmering under moonlight, and I realize that I'm not yet experienced enough to use someone for sex. But Sea Horse is heaving his big chest, his lustful eyes stroking the naked contours of my perfect body, his penis pointing down but still stiff as a shiny new rifle. He says in a deep, violent voice, "I ought to fuck you right here. Make you suck my dick."

"Is that what you are—a rapist?"

"You don't know me, bitch. You've been playing with

fire, so whatever I am—that's what you asked for."

He covers me like a blanket, and even though I'm six feet tall, his height still makes me feel small. I refuse to accept his mouth in a kiss. The harder he presses his chest and knees and penis against my nakedness, the more I freeze and slither our bodies out of sync, making it obvious that he will have no choice but to take me by force.

"If you try to fight, I could fuck up your face," he whispers in my ear menacingly.

"That's why I'm not fighting, you son of a bitch."

"You *want* me to rape you!"

I look straight up in his eyes and say with all the sincerity I can muster, "I'm begging you . . . please don't."

"Why have you been playing games?"

"Because . . . I've never been with a black man before."

Amazingly, that makes him back up. He stares at me and says, "I should have known. You African supermodels are all known for being the white man's whore."

"Your wife is white!"

"That's different," he says, beating his chest. "I'm a man!"

"Oh please! Doesn't one of your lyrics say that we Africans need to get rid of the King Kongs? Well look at yourself, Kong!"

His voice thunders now. "Millicent is not white—I know her, she's just a woman!"

"Well, the only man I ever loved is white. And just like Millicent, he's English. But I've never had sex with a black man before, and since I found you so incredibly sexy and since you're already married to several women, I figured I could use you for sex. But I couldn't go through with it."

"You said *loved*. So you're not with this white man now?"

It's as though his complete opinion of me is riding on my answer. And for some reason, I want so much for him to forgive me and like me, so I lie and say, "No, we're not together."

He doesn't respond.

I continue, "He never introduced me to his family, and he cheats, so I had to break it off."

"You never did answer my question," he finally says. "Do you ever pray like your people to the ocean?"

"Do you ever pray like *your* people to the sky?"

"No, God would never listen to me. I've done too many sins. But since you're an Ajowan woman, I thought from the moment I saw you that maybe I could get you to pray for me."

How to Pray for a Happy Ending

I have an awful lot to hide from people. So although we will leave this night believing that we'll never see each other again, I feel compelled to present only an illusion of myself to him. At the lagoon shore he builds a fire so I can go about pretending I know how to pray to the ocean—I am filled with the sadness of knowing that while Sea Horse is someone's child, I am not a child, but a duplicate.

In spite of this, I take his hand and ask him as Nana Oluchi once asked me, "Have you ever been taught the correct way to pray?"

"No," he shakes his head. "What is the correct way to pray?"

"With the knowledge that nothing in this world is as it was meant to be."

"Pray for me," he says low but urgent. "I'm about to enter a bad oven. I need the ancestors of every tribe on my side, because I'm about to wrestle with scorpions and snakes—I'm going to fight for the people!"

Somehow, with our government's Spy Control watching his every move at the resort, I know what he means. A shudder goes down my spine because the stereotype I have is that people like him are known for self-destructing.

"Pray for me, beautiful sister, to deliver Africa from the bondage of her greedy black army dogs and fat stupid dictators. Pray for my journey to yield a good crop. Pray for every drop of my blood that goes into the ground to rise up a new son. Pray for all of us—we, the true Africans—we who go with the landscape."

I hold his hand and I posit us in the direction of the white moon over the sea. I pray for his safety.

"Amen," we say. Then Sea Horse explains to me that he originally hated rap music and sang traditional songs; but the white record company executives were only looking to sign Africans who could rap. So he taught himself to mimic the flow and style of the black Americans he'd been able to hear on cassette.

Then he begins to sing with the smoothest, most soul-tingling voice, masculine and rich as tobacco. He sings of the blisters on our people's hands and of the illnesses that women get cutting cassava. He sings about being born and leaving this earth with one's whole life taxed by the government. Of course, because I come from a laboratory and not from the people, I know very little about the Africa he talks about. I have been sheltered and raised in relative ignorance.

When we part, I hate to say goodbye.

"Goodbye, beautiful sister," he offers. "You give good prayer. It was better than sex."

LONDON

It's several months later and I'm sitting in the back of James's Daimler as the chauffer takes me to do a layout for Brazzaville Vineyard's Wine. Opened on my knee is the latest issue of M magazine with the completed feature article about me. In America and Europe, the article seems to have made a big splash. I am now receiving offers for supporting roles in what my agent calls "arthouse prestige films." I reread my favorite thing that I said in the entire interview: *Beauty is when you look like your own people. That way, everyone is beautiful.*

The car is passing Big Ben, and all of a sudden the announcer on the radio is saying: *"You crazy blokes and bints have gotten biscuit-whipped over his sensational rap hits, but now he's gone and made a love ballad—it's number five in the UK this week—King Sea Horse Twee singing 'One Night Angel.'"*

His voice covers me with goosebumps and I think I might pee on myself:

I found a girl so black she doesn't need clothes
I tried to find where I left her, but nobody knows
I'm hardly the perfect mate, I have an awful lot to hide and
Now I guess it's too late

But just for a moment—she gave my heart an earthquake
I was loved by that girl . . . the one who goes
the one who goes
with the landscape

The Heat of African November

American and European guests figured it was mildewed mesquite they smelled over dance music and the clinking of champagne glasses at state parties, or perhaps animal fat wrapped in gasoline rags that had accidentally fallen into Colonel Botha's barbeque pits. But no, it was human flesh that they smelled—the crackling burn of nappy crotches and scalps wafting on the night breeze to arouse their palates. The charred bones and roasted guts of journalists and editors who'd published the wrong news stories, village mothers who'd sung the wrong chants, desperately unemployed fathers, uncles, and older brothers of starving little sisters who'd come beating on the double doors of the presidential palace demanding liberation.

These were the Africans whose bodies slow-cooked just yards away from the hoop skirts and shiny black loafers that crowded Colonel Botha's dancefloor.

—Euggi Damel, *Negro Journal*, 1968

DRIVE SLOW

The reason that I'd so nervously clung to the door handle in the back of the Mercedes as we coasted along from DakCrete Airport to the state-sponsored ball at Yaw Ibrahim's presidential palace was because I'd been learning the hard way that it's the insecure people, the ones with so-called low self-esteem, who actually rule this world. They not only set the style and bring about change, but they can make the most immature and destructive behavior socially accepted as cool or normal. They can take a perfectly natural human being and reduce that person to the rags they're wearing or the religion they don't understand or the mush and water in their bellies—and, in kind, whatever is touched by the insecure becomes unstable as well. I was sure that's what had been happening to me all along.

"Identify yourselves," ordered a black soldier at the palace gate with a machine gun over his shoulder, as he leaned his head into the driver's window of the car and glanced around.

"Supermodel Eternity Frankenheimer," my chauffeur said, handing the soldier my invitation from Spy Control.

The car began moving again, my eyes fixated on the long stretches of melancholy baobab trees and dusty red road. I shuddered at the thought of being anywhere near President Yaw Ibrahim or any member of my country's government. But then to decline the invitation to so important an event might have made them suspicious of my political loyalties and could've caused them to harass my mother's clinic, or put me through hell whenever I tried to enter or leave the country.

Slowly, like a casket on wheels, my Mercedes glided forward, the feast of the nation opening up before my eyes as I saw fireworks delivering blue, pink, and green flower sparks from behind the presidential palace—which in our country, like in many African countries, is called the White House. And out in front of the White House hung the flag of West Cassavaland, flowing majestically from the fourth-story balcony, flapping across the Greek columns of the first-floor veranda before resting in all its five-colored splendor against the grassy knoll; the color green for the cassava crops, ocean-blue for the Ajowan tribe, solid black for the God tribe (now called the Oluchi), blood-red for the armed forces, and canary-yellow representing the Pogo Metis Signare mulatto elite.

Chained around the White House as a kind of human rope were soldiers bearing machine guns. The huge double doors of the palace were open wide with a red carpet leading up the marble porch and into the foyer where massive French and Portuguese chandeliers hung from a twenty-foot ceiling, while in the foreground there was a great ceremony of what is called the national class (the dark-skinned black majority), beating bongos, slicing coconuts open with machetes, and performing extravagant tribal dances for the benefit of fascinated white foreign dignitaries while calling out one of the most traditional election-time chants known to West Africa: "*He killed my pa, he killed my ma . . . but I will vote for him!*"

The drum orchestra filled up the landscape with an

earthquakelike *BOOM!* as several soldiers happily fired gunshots in sync with it. Then the people chanted again: *"He killed my pa, he killed my ma . . . but I will vote for him!"*

"Let the Gods be born!" sang a regiment of dancing Oluchi women, to which the men hollered the traditional reply, *"You go put die!?"* which was followed again by *BOOM!* Then from the second- and third-story balconies, tuxedoed and ball-gowned white, yellow, and tobacco-brown party guests sipped crème de cacao from Ming Wa tea cups and leisurely flicked the ashes from their thinly rolled marijuana cigarettes onto the festival of Africans below.

My Mercedes came to a stop in front of the White House, and it seemed as though a million eyes fell across its spiffy exterior in anticipation of who it might be carrying. I truly was scared to get out, but then a valet wearing white gloves opened my door, and I heard someone announce over the loudspeakers, *"One of our nation's most beautiful daughters—Miss Eter—"*

Before he could get my name out, the crowd thundered—their love and excitement literally washing over my body like a vibe-shower. As my vermillion Dior heels swung out of the car and crunched down against the dirt, it felt exhilarating to realize for the first time that I had "made it" in the eyes of my people, and that I was now of that tiny class that meant something good and hopeful to the masses of insecure people in my country.

With the heat of an African November night completely cocooning my skin in a fiery blanket from heaven, the valet gave to me the customary Oluchi welcome, "No evil?"

"Only goodness," I replied. I waved as democratically

as I could to those who were cheering me and peered up at the white-tuxedoed, red-carnation men standing around the palace entrance—and noticed immediately a very handsome but menacing Pogo Metis Signare.

He was banana-yellow with a ski-slope Eurocentric nose, dark Ajowan jungle lips, and the wavy hair of a Spaniard. He was staring right into me as though he'd been waiting all his life for me to get there—and in the next two hours he would alter my life's course forever.

Should I start believing in God now? After all, here is the antithesis of everything my scientific upbringing had ever raised me to believe, the irrefutable larger-than-life coincidence, what I suppose Christians would call a miracle. Yet I wasn't surprised. You see, I knew in that moment that *you* would be born.

PASSION'S NAKED EYE

My dear son . . . In retrospect, there will be those who claim that I never deserved the love of Sea Horse and that I was just a whorish bitch, the worst kind of African woman—a womanist—but rubbish! The God's truth is, I possessed the most death-defying soul and didn't even know it. One life simply hadn't done it justice. And until that night, I had never really understood what an African is, or what the land is, or what a woman's purpose really is after she gets done dismissing the bullshit lies that men ordain and distribute out of their insecurity. I was very, very young, believing that I had no soul. Then right there, in the clearest moment of all my moments, I knew that *you* were coming.

I wasn't sure when or how you would be conceived.

It never occurred to me to even think about which of my men would be the one to impregnate me—but as I walked up that red carpet, I became caught up in what I now call the Moment of God—the moment of coincidence. I didn't believe it, but it was real. I was being summoned by the stare of my own brother, Tiberius Perrina.

Tiberius.

At seven years old he'd watched helplessly as I was kicked to death in the streets of DakCrete, and then later lifted away by the arms of Stevedore, carried off never to be seen again. So to find him again was utter affirmation of my purpose in a second life. And so it is for you, my son, that I've been telling this story. Tiberius Perrina, the undeniable symbol of coincidence and the possibility that God is real, was to become the homing pigeon—the messenger.

You Go Put Die?

After I'd been bashed in the head with a sockful of gravel and stuffed into the trunk of Tiberius's automobile, the air leaking in as we sped across the African savannah awakened me. And though I wasn't yet aware of the identity of my kidnapper, I backtracked in my mind, trying to retrace where I'd been and what had been happening.

A trickle of blood running past my ear and across my nose reminded me of sauntering into the sunken great room of President Yaw Ibrahim just in time to witness his tall but stout figure standing in the center of a circle of about fifty people, mostly men, as his voice projected across the room hyperbolically, "Here's to our mother, the mighty West Cassavaland. May her light be the light of the world!"

Clink.

One of the few African women allowed in the room, a maid, handed me a glass of champagne as she passed by. I felt uncomfortable because a presidential aide a few feet behind me was explaining to people why I had been invited by the White House. "She's become world famous despite her color," he half-whispered apologetically. It was embarrassing and hurtful.

In our country, you don't see a charcoal woman mingling in ballrooms with the yellow class, the Pogo Metis Signare.

Of course, had I been a charcoal-complexioned male, no one would have batted an eye. But for a female so absolute in blackness to be present as a "peer," it generated alarm. I copped an attitude. Then, just as the yellow Africans began rolling their eyes, in walked the mysterious mulatto, Tiberius Perrina. His stare homed in on me as though I were some prized cobra rising from a basket.

I sipped my champagne, definitely remembering him from somewhere. But who was he, and why was he affecting me so strongly? Out of fear, I refused his stare and convinced myself that his aim was probably to rape me, as so frequently happened to unescorted women at these balls. And with that, I dismissed him, instead pretending to listen intently as President Yaw Ibrahim capped off his nomination speech with the dire statement: "You can either agree with me . . . or be wrong."

A few of the white men chuckled, but the majority of us knew he was dead serious. Our nation was run by greedy, shiny-faced, chocolate fudge–colored criminals, some of them like President Yaw Ibrahim professing Christianity, others Islam—but for all of them, money was their true religion; the white man and the Arab man their Gods, foreign women or young boys their secret sexual pursuits, and Western imperialism, Arab imperialism, and Chinese imperialism the only understanding through which they could gain validation. They were no different than our final European president during colonial times, the infamous blue-eyed flesh-eating Colonel Botha, who'd been forced by the World Court to sign us over to independence, thus granting our first democratic elections. But all for naught, of course, as the people's elected choices had been quickly forced out in coups by the national army—coups that were funded by invisible outside power brokers with faces and identities that couldn't be proven.

West Cassavaland, like so many African nations, just couldn't get its act together. The white ruling colonialists moved out, and the tiny mulatto elite (barely numbering fifty thousand in the whole nation) braced in horror at the thought of being ruled by the very blacks they'd been bred to look down upon. The pure-black majority found that their sudden freedom tasted like bile, as poverty and lack of leadership spiraled out of control, entombing their dreams of having a real country down into the rotten ground, without seed, so that nothing could grow. And in all these years, even with the land deals our government struck with the oil conglomerates, nothing did grow.

President Yaw Ibrahim, a former general of the army who couldn't do math and didn't believe that white men had landed on the moon, but rather that they had landed on a studio soundstage in an elaborate world hoax, was soon smiling broadly and thanking all of us at the ball for his imminent reelection. He'd already ruled more than a decade, to the point where he owned an island near the one that Marlon Brando had owned and kept a Tudor mansion with a white mistress in London and a chateau with a white mistress in the south of France. His boiled orange–colored African wife, First Lady Marionette, dripped in diamonds and spent most of her time poolside, ordering her maids about and boasting that all fourteen of their children were attending university in the West. Not a thing about their lives was in common with the masses, yet no matter how the Cassavan people suffered and begged for change, Yaw Ibrahim the Black was always elected.

Dutifully, we each got in line to meet the president.

"Good job," said the American oil company executive up front, shaking hands and patting Ibrahim while a British ambassador proclaimed, "Your leadership has been very beneficial to our vision for Africa. You're an excellent president."

I looked around, wondering about King Sea Horse Twee and half-expecting to see him somewhere in the room, since Ibrahim had made it a point to invite any West Cassavan who'd become famous at something. I saw football players, recording stars, and people who'd run in the Olympics. But nowhere in sight was our nation's biggest superstar—and then, amazingly, it was my turn.

"Greetings, dear president," I said graciously. I curtsied and bowed. The president nodded, smiling dismissively. Then the first lady shook my hand, commented that I looked even more stunning in person than I did on magazine covers, and that was that.

I continued down the carpet past the soldiers and out the back patio doors, my entire body relieved by the warmth of the night air as the tumbling bossa nova of the jazz band played in the palace garden where Africa's richest politely socialized.

"Sister . . . may I have this dance?"

When I turned around I wanted to faint. The face of the handsome mulatto was close enough to touch, his astonished cognac-colored eyes calling out beyond the nakedness of his birth, as right away I remembered every inch of him! *Tiberius*, my brother.

Dear God! In my first life as Orisha, I had been the one to pull him from my mother while she begged God that he come out stillborn. I had been the one who changed his diaper until he was potty-trained, had braided people's hair to afford banana for his porridge, and had held his crying, shaking body across my shoulder when our mother refused to.

This man was not a member of the elite Pogo Metis Signare, to which almost all of West Cassavaland's yellow people belonged—he was my little brother from my other life; a rape baby who had stuck out like a sore thumb among the poor black inner-city Ajowans. The last child of my mother, Nonni.

Yes, her name came back to me . . . Ma Nonni. *Oh my God!* Our mother, the dollmaker!

I almost reached out and grabbed him into my arms, almost held and kissed him. Vividly, the dollmaker walked into my field of remembrance as though she'd

never been gone. Her head full of plaits and her skin
the deep, dark reddish-brown of coffee beans; her jolly
cheekbones and lips full of syrup, and the flat, wide
nose that Pa called "sexy."

"Orisha," the mulatto man whispered through trembling lips. He thought I was Orisha. But then again, what
else could he think? "I've seen you on the magazine covers, modeling. It is me, Tiberius, your baby brother . . .
I'm a man now."

I could scarcely stand to be looked at once more by
the same eyes that had witnessed me being kicked to
death. Yet through his eyes I could recall the dolls lined
up around the walls of the tiny thatch-roofed house
where cracks in the narrow street outside, wide as rubber leaves, kept a constant traffic jam about which all of
Pa and Ma Bedee's children had grown up dust-covered
and laughing, shiny black as Arabian horses while we
played jump rope or hide-and-seek or went to the field
of the Christ Church to watch the Ajowan boys play
football.

"My leader wanted someone else to fetch you," Tiberius was saying, excitedly. "One of our spies, but I
said no—send me! I knew her before she was the Second
Moon Cosmetics girl. She won't be afraid to come with
me—send me!"

On purpose, I looked at him as though he were crazy.

I had been thirty-three when Tiberius was born. My
pa, a rugged blue-black factory foreman named Easter
Bedee, had been locked up two years earlier over some
comment he'd made at a borough meeting regarding oil
drilling and tribes being forced off their land, and had
ended up dying in the jail from pneumonia. Of course,

he'd never allowed Mother to work outside the home, and because my brothers had jobs as well, she'd never needed to. But once Pa was dead and Ma Nonni let Kiongo take a wife and sent the other boys off for trade schooling, she'd taken up going door to door to sell the beautiful dolls she made as a hobby. And it was in one of the wealthier neighborhoods where the European diplomats and other foreigners lived that she'd been brutally raped one afternoon while showing her dolls to a Lebanese father and son.

Out of it had come Tiberius, who Ma Nonni gave the last name Perrina in a desperate attempt at class jockeying. She would tell people that his father was Italian and not Arab.

In my beforehand as Orisha Bedee, I could never have forgotten the sight of Ma Nonni's white-skinned, blue marble–eyed plastic dolls, objects that she'd spent most of her life creating, stacked up outside the house as she'd ordered my brothers to take them to the woods and burn them till they became a single mass of plastic. Nor could I forget the vile disgust on her face every time she looked at baby Tiberius.

"Ma Nonni, he's just an innocent baby."

"Then you raise him. His life is a curse that the dolls put on me. Your father said this would happen—me playing with white dolls all my life. He said they'd find a way to come through me if I didn't put them down!"

Everyone on the block had taken turns raising the little ink-haired yellow baby, including me and my sisters Yandi and Wilma, but mainly those African women in the neighborhood who'd always fantasized about being light-skinned and having what Africans call "Been-to" hair, of a Caucasian texture, and many of them were bleachers and swallowers, so they worshipped and spoiled Tiberius rotten. But even so, with all that love and adoration from so many Ajowans, he was still rejected by Ma Nonni at every passing birthday, and in doing so, she literally destroyed whoever Tiberius was meant to be and left in his place a sad, sensitive little yellow boy, forever in search of his identity and severely traumatized by the fact that he could never be sure if anyone loved him for who he was without his yellow skin and Been-to hair.

To my astonishment, Tiberius worshipped the ground Ma Nonni walked on; because humans are known to obsess over those who reject them. It shocked everyone that he loved her more than any other woman in the Ajowan community.

"I've become an activist!" he told me that evening at the White House, his hands on my shoulders. "Like you, Orisha, I speak out against the Bastardization!"

The Bastardization. Just as Americans say the Reconstruction or the New Deal, he uttered the common Afrikaans term that was used in South Africa, Namibia, and other colonies to refer to when mixed races started officially being called "Bastars Elite." In our country, because Spaniards and Portuguese had mixed with some of us before the British invasion of 1640, the Bastars class renamed themselves Pogo Metis Signare in 1720 and proclaimed their allegiance to some unseen Fatherland in lieu of the Motherland (Africa) they felt ashamed of. They started the Democratic Fatherland Party at the all-mulatto township of Port Elizabeth in 1748, and embraced what we call the Bastardization as a cure for African inferiority. The original thinking went that they would breed an African superclass, the "Talented Tenth," and destroy the image of Cassavans as savages.

I tell you, I could hardly take it, the memories flooding into my head like rain off the sea. Orisha Bedee's memories. I saw myself amongst that circle of Africans who secretly gathered each week in Mr. Kingston's basement, all of us wearing solid-black armbands with a splotch of red in the middle, as Brother Kingston educated us about the two ages, the Twee-Sankofa Madal and the Bastardization.

Twee-Sankofa Madal, of course, means "the paradise"—the world that existed not only before the white invaders, but before our kings began trading with the Arab Muslims. The world when our greatest founding father, the trickster warrior-cum-deity, Twee Obatala, had blessed the sea for the Ajowans, the sky for the God tribe, and had filled the African jungles and rivers with an abundance of tropical wonders, a richness of natural resources, and a never-ending supply of food, space, and freedom.

Everyone—*everyone who lived in paradise times*, Brother Kingston taught us—was black. All kings, all queens, all griots of the spiritual world, all children, the living and the dead—*everyone*—had been truly African, possessing Obatala's wooly hair and thickly sculptured facial features. The flesh of the coastal sea-worshipping Ajowans had come in shades that ran from blue-black to burnt chocolate to coffee-bean brown to light chocolate and tobacco, while the mountain- and jungle-dwelling God tribe had been wholly charcoal—some with a silvery sheen and others with a dusty matte finish, but all of them tall and royal-looking with glorious charcoal complexions.

"There was no yellow," Brother Kingston had said in a calm but venomous tone. "Not until the invaders came and sought to conquer and control us. And who among us, anywhere in Africa, can claim to be unaware of the white and Arab man's single greatest tactic for dividing and conquering African people? The tactic of raping our women and thereby separating us from our ancestors by literally seizing and diluting the blood in our veins. The colonization of blood instead of land; the *forced* bastard-ization that has historically allowed white invaders to rule African people through a buffer race that is called by our name but is truly just an extension of the European hand!"

As the basement activists applaud in Tiberius's eyes, I heard my biracial brother presently saying, "I have joined the Twee-Sankofa Madal—*the paradise*, Orisha. I am now truly a black man, an African! I am aware of the colonizer's tricks to separate us!"

His conviction and passion for what he was saying both startled and impressed me. He held up the same pamphlets I'd once handed out to bleachers and swallowers—illustrated pamphlets that pointed out the physical dangers caused by skin bleaching, while at the same time calling for nationalistic pride and appreciation of ancestral purity to strengthen and unify blacks through self-love and self-acceptance. This was why I'd been called "The Racist." It broke my heart as I realized that in a nation where most Pogo Metis Signare still demanded separation from the black African majority, my brother was willing to kill himself in order to be black enough.

I found it hard to look him in the eyes and say what I was about to say. I tightened my bowels, rooted my feet to the patio floor, and solemnly declared, "My name is not Orisha." Tiberius fell back on his haunches, speechless, as I added, "And I don't know what you're talking about."

"But you know me—you have to! I'm *Tiberius*! You're the only person who ever truly loved me. You loved me with all your heart!" Tears rolled down his face as the very fiber of his being pleaded with me to remember him—yet the memories of who I'd been were too much for me to swallow. It seemed as though I could hear the person I had loved more than anyone—my father, Easter Bedee—demanding to know why his thirty-three-year-old daughter was a spinster. Why I was always marching, organizing, handing out pamphlets.

No, I couldn't go back. This was just too fucking much.

"Somehow you're much younger than when you died," Tiberius was saying, "but it's you. You practically raised me until that day when the bleachers and swallowers—"

"Get away from me!" I jerked his hands off my body and shouted, "I don't know you! . . . I don't! I don't!"

Tiberius desperately ignored the people staring at us because of my outburst and said, "Before mother died . . ."

Before mother died!

"She saw you in the fashion magazines. I brought her every one of them I could find, and she said it too— *That's Orisha! Come back to life.* And now that I'm standing before you, I have no doubt in mind as to who—"

Ka-plapp! I slapped the taste out of his mouth. "Shut the fuck up!" I hissed low, sounding just like the little possessed girl from *The Exorcist*. Then I turned and ran, finding a staircase that went up to a huge crowded bathroom where I quickly powdered my nose with the rest of the women.

THREE NIPPLES, DEAR EYE

When the car stopped and I heard my kidnapper get out from the driver's side, I felt it again—*that you would be born*. Because of that I lost all fear, realizing that the kidnapper might be Tiberius. As he popped open the trunk and the roundest, pearliest white moon shone down upon me, I squinted, relieved that it was indeed my brother. But then I got frightened again when he pulled his shirt over his head, revealing his tattooed chest as he explained, "I'm sorry I had to chloroform you, but my leader ordered that you be fetched."

"Who's this leader you keep talking about?"

He hoisted my body from the trunk and said, "King Sea Horse Twee."

Dear Eye, of course I was shocked, outraged, and strangely titillated to hear that it was Sea Horse who had me abducted, and that I was about to be reunited with him. But the thing that left me speechless was the sight of the Bedee family's secret; the birthmark on my brother's bare chest that I'd hidden from Ma Nonni all the days I'd known her—his third nipple. He had a normal one on the right side of his chest, but then two on the other side—one an inch and a half south of his left clavicle, the other a quarter-inch below and to the side of that one—with both of them completely out of alignment with the right nipple.

As Tiberius continued raving about Sea Horse—"The greatest warrior trickster, the greatest Twee since Fela Kuti, since Steve Biko, since Malcolm X"—my stare became riveted to the beautiful tattoo that was apparently supposed to hide his freakish left nipples. In fact, the upper nipple had been disguised to form the head of the green-and-red Sea Horse that rose just above a dagger—but no matter, I knew they were there.

He slammed the trunk shut. And as he carried me around and propped me up in the front seat, I realized that we had left the hot November night winds of the African savannah and were pointed toward the cool opening locks of the Katanga Jungle. Staring as deep as he could see inside my eyes, Tiberius kissed me very gently on the mouth. Then he said, "I had a sister once who looked like you. You're the reincarnation of her."

I bristled. "There's no such thing as reincarnation."

Tiberius ignored me. "I was seven. At the exact moment when her heart stopped beating, I felt it stop, and her spirit brushed right past my shoulder—I wanted to die too."

"But you would have been disappointed," I told him, "because there's no such thing as death. Our living in this world is not life; not the real life."

GOD AND SATAN ARE BLACK—BURNT BLACK

Dear Eye, it would mean so much to me if I could see this night forever. But the more I memorize it, the more it changes, until each time I recall it—the further away I get from when it was real:

. . . In the jungle where the road stopped black as

pitch, Tiberius turned off the engine and the headlights. Moments later, we were met by seven African men, both Ajowan and Oluchi, a few of them carrying flashlights and rifles while others bore machetes and geranium torches to ward off mosquitoes. Tiberius informed me that we would have to walk the rest of the way to the stone ruins of Hembadoon, which had been the capital of the Oluchi people before slavery days, back when they'd been called the God tribe.

I took off my shoes, hiked up my evening gown, and held my baby brother's hand as the men led us across a narrow path of smooth, cool earth. All the way down it was like walking on dry lacquered mud, and when we reached the bottom of the hill and shot off the guns to scare away crocodiles in what I soon realized was an everglade, we boarded a long canoe and began rowing across the scariest black marsh until we reached open water. In the blink of an eye, we were being pulled into the radiance of Lake Mona Lisa, which before colonialism had been called Lake Ambi in honor of the God ruler King Katanga's wife, Queen Ambi. I quickly realized that ours was not the only canoe. The black lake, quiet as it was, was full of flickering torches and flashlights searching the water—and all along the shores of the jungle, as I looked back over my shoulder, I saw that people were coming from everywhere.

"Don't look back!" scolded one of the Oluchi men sitting behind me. "You'll wake up God Sakhr!"

Very briefly, Tiberius explained to me, "One afternoon our people's greatest warrior, Twee Obatala, was walking down a road with his warrior son, Twee Egubo. Suddenly, the sky over the road turned dark. Up ahead of them, peering from behind a tree, was God Sakhr—Satan—ten feet tall and black as tar with twelve dangling penises and the flickering tongue of a snake. As the warriors nodded to God Sakhr and passed him by, Obatala warned his son, 'He will follow us in the road now, all the way to our destination, but as long as you don't look back at him while it's nighttime, he can't harm you.' On and on the warriors walked with God Sakhr close behind. But unfortunately, feeling and smelling the labored breathing of Sakhr against his neck for several miles, Egubo found himself unable to resist looking back. And when he did, his father, choking back tears, could only stare straight ahead and walk on without him."

Looking forward, it seemed that our canoe and countless other torch-lit boats had sailed across the swishing darkness a good forty-five minutes before we detected the pungent burn of a marijuana field as it dueled with eucalyptus, peppermint, and peanut oil (antimosquito smoke) for dominance. Soon we could hear the faint thump of recorded music being blasted from speakers—the timeless jazz of Ethiopia's Mulatu Astatke turning into America's KRS-One, Public Enemy, and MC Lyte, before dipping into the lake and rising back up as the soulful voices of the Emperor Baaba Maal, Burning Spear, Stella Chiweshe, and Angie Stone. I smelled a dang-boy African barbeque cooking in ground holes with coal, stones, and dried leaves and began to hear the chattering laughter of ooh-Luck (black folk) socializing as the beautifully hypnotic voice of world music's undisputed Queen of African Song, Oumou Sangare, rang out and drew us in like a mother's prayer.

Before long, we could more than smell the burning field. We could see the coast, the rage of orange flames flickering over monkey- and cockatoo-infested sook trees. We could see the off and on of lightning bugs and could feel the vibrations of the coming land—white ash blowing across our bodies and faces as Oumou Sangare's lush vocals turned into Faada Freddy's mesmerizing flow, a lyrical cook-down with Daara J, and then Daara J, too smooth, erupting like smoke from a bong as it gave way to the genius "Gis Gis" of Ifang Bondi.

"Hell fuck'n yeah!" came the shouts of unseeable black men along the shoreline brush. The females shouted back, "You go put die!"

"Hold on tight!" Tiberius warned, and just as he said it our canoe crash-slid against a solid wall of blackness. Two of the men jumped into the shallow coast water and held the boat steady as Tiberius got out and carried me to the upper dune landing where other groups of people were gathering to be admitted down a road guarded by makeshift soldiers. As Tiberius let go of me, I heard an Ajowan mother imploring her children, "Do not look back!" then felt stricken as two white women were physically blocked by the road guards and told, "No Caucasoids are welcome here."

"Isgom-uh da eh Sulu," one of the women responded, respectfully.

But her speaking the Oluchi language only infuriated the men more. They shouted emphatically, "This is a family meeting for ooh-Luck only! Get back on your boat!"

"Go back to Europe!" people in the crowd echoed angrily, and as the two white women paid an outrageous sum of money for the boy who'd rowed them across the lake to take them back, I nearly came to tears thinking about my own white mother and how deeply it would have hurt me had she been turned away like that.

"Tiberius!" shrieked a young woman's voice. The most wondrously petite and pretty chocolate-skinned Oluchi girl came dashing into his arms, their faces butting like two kissing fish and her cute little onion booty wiggling as if she were a puppy whose master had just returned. My brother stopped and announced proudly, "Orisha—uhhh, I mean, Eternity . . . I want you to meet my wife, the beautiful Chiamaka."

"Well, how do you do?" I smiled in surprise. Chiamaka gushed about my celebrity, chirping away as she shook my hand. Then, as if remembering that Tiberius was standing there, she said abruptly, "The revolution is here now, sister. We're going to be rid of Yaw Ibrahim and the Democratic Fatherland Party for good! We're going to make Sea Horse the new president!"

I'd scarcely had time to form a reply when another beautiful young African woman, this one a Muslim wearing a silk ivory burka, walked right up to me and stared into my face as though it were a mask that she wanted to rip off the bones.

Startled, I put my hand to my throat, my engagement ring sparkling against my velvety dark complexion as Chiamaka stopped chirping to say, "Oh, Tasso, here she is—the one Sea Horse wrote the song about."

"I know who she is," Tasso intoned. "I've seen the magazines."

"Eternity Frankenheimer, meet Tasso Twee—wife of Sea Horse."

Again, I felt stricken. I didn't know what to say.

"I'm his God-given wife," Tasso explained. "We were born and raised together in the same village. We got married after he finished schooling. We have six sons and two daughters."

I couldn't bring myself to meet her gaze. But I did manage to say, "My God, you're so young and beautiful to have had all those children."

"Millicent York says that too," she replied sarcastically. Just as I began wondering whether the "no whites" rule would be set aside for Millicent, Tasso added, "But his white cow won't be here tonight. Only his African wives."

Knowing that Tasso was Sea Horse's only African wife, I searched her face for confirmation of what I thought she was implying, but her irises turned to butcher knives, the sharp tips of them glinting.

Then Tiberius remarked, "I didn't know his black American wife was coming tonight."

"She's not," Tasso said. "Only his *African* wives."

And with that, Tiberius and Chiamaka looked at me with a silly hopefulness.

KNOWING

Now we entered the road of humming Cassavans. The longer we walked, the hotter the moon got, and the more it became a march. The men were draped in beautifully flowing boubous, walking erect, black and purposeful; the women were equally black, their soulfully thick-featured faces committed to whatever their men endeavored as they wore intricate multicolored tunics, sported natural African hairstyles, and carried babies on their backs and baskets atop their heads. Though I thought we looked impressive coming down the road by the hundreds, we could hear the thunder of thousands more who had gathered where the music was coming from, their voices drowning out the blaring sound of the Fugees, as they chanted, "No-MO White House . . . No-MO White House!"

Abruptly curving through jungle and the charred rubble walls of what had once been Hembadoon, capital city of the Gods, we came upon the spotlight; a brightly lit ocean of shimmering Ajowans and Oluchis, waving and chanting while up on the concert stage sat Sea Horse, his legs arrogantly cocked open as he lounged on his throne surrounded by his hip-hop entourage and took drags from a marijuana stick.

Dear Eye, rage filled me up! Black evil-bitch rage!

The nerve of this motherfucker—treating me like some video hoochie he could just snatch out of a party! I swear on a stack of Bibles that if I hadn't been so shocked about being reunited with my brother, I wouldn't have stood there so agreeably. And if I'd had any clue what the crowd was going to end up doing to me that night, I would have run for my life and not stopped until I'd swum across the lake and made it all the way to my mother's clinic.

But I stayed, and at some point the music stopped. Onstage a group of topless Oluchi river women walked up to a microphone and quieted the crowd with a sovereign ululation.

Tasso, who had left us and taken her place next to Sea Horse onstage, came to the microphone and spoke with an eloquent humbleness: "My husband needs only ten thousand signatures to register his name on the ballot for president. As a Cassava woman, a Muslim, and the mother of eight children, I remind you that this is not Europe; this is not the Fatherland. This is Africa, the *Motherland!*"

The masses went wild, interrupting Tasso with chants of *"Golu! Golu! Golu!"*

She shouted over them into the microphone, "And let us establish tonight the first ever United Nationalist Motherland Party!"

Behind Tasso, as the people continued yelling and cheering, the topless river women raised a massive red flag over their heads—and in the center of it were two Black Power fists, one representing the Ajowans and the other representing the Oluchis.

A big-screen television was then rolled out to the edge of the stage and a microphone placed at its speaker as the nearly white face of the leader of the Pogo Metis Signare, Walter Wasoon, flashed across it. *"The key to eliminating racism is for all people to melt together as one,"* he said. *"We who are mulatto Cassavans have always understood that. It's about evolving into a kinder, gentler Africa, a place for everyone, a brighter future!"*

On the screen, you could see the packed auditorium at the Union of World Bankers convention enthusiastically applauding Wasoon as he concluded, *"Colonialism is gone, but without the white man, Africa would be lost. So please help us to keep evolving by continuing to sponsor President Yaw Ibrahim the Black, and the African Democratic Fatherland Party!"*

Europeans, Jews, Arabs, Asians, Africans, Latinos. They all cheered on the television as Sea Horse, from his big chair, lifted up a .38-caliber pistol and—*PeeYOON!*—no more picture tube.

The ooh-Luck of the jungle, including me, cheered so loudly it was deafening. Then with grace and charisma, Sea Horse Twee stood before us at last and said, "My brothers and sisters, my mothers and fathers, dear ancestors and the unborn . . . both God and Satan are pure black. Both God and Satan are the two halves of one complete thought. Both good and evil are the ingredients of the human being—and we, my people, the Africans, are the first human beings on earth, and the most good and the most evil that has ever graced life. We are the saviors for all who need saving, because it is us and only us who can grow the nappy hair of God from our scalps—no other race has this crown!

"Every natural resource on earth, every type of wealth, beauty, and wonder—it exists in Africa and exists abundantly, as though leftover from a great paradise, and only *we* can save Africa. We, who before the Muslim and Christian invaders forced their religions on us, were members of the two churches of our ancestors—the sun and the river. We, with the black skin, the thick lips, the wide noses, the hair like God's—*we who go with the landscape*—we who should be asking ourselves, Why do we need white men and Arab men and China men and mulattoes to legislate and dictate and govern Mother Africa when it's only the Africans who can save Africa? Why do we need the Pogo-niggers who inhabit the White House to represent us by lining their pockets with foreign aid while doing nothing for the people, nothing for the land?

"How many times have we been told by the mulattoes of Port Elizabeth that the only way to end race is to get rid of the black people and become mixed ourselves? How many times have we been removed from our own land, erased from our own stories and songs, shut up from our own truth, and evicted . . . *evicted* from the love our ancestors shared? How many times has the revolution come? And yet still today there is no Africa for the African. No leadership, no justice, no wealth, no power, no freedom, no glory, and very little self-respect.

"We turn on the television and only our suffering is recorded by the white man's cameras—our poverty, our hunger, our disease. Not only exaggerated, but the *cause* of our downfall is never truthfully explained. And while the white man films himself saving us, medicating us, feeding and protecting us, the black man is portrayed as a loser who can't navigate his own land, can't love or feed his family, and can't stand up as an African in the image, fully human, that God created him in. He's just a backward nigger in a dying, stinking, rotten paradise—*that everybody wants*."

OFFERING

I was to be the offering and didn't know it.

Sinful as insanity, I felt so ashamed about the wetness that glazed my vagina as I watched Sea Horse give voice to the voiceless, commanding the minds and imaginations of thousands. Though I was so far from the stage that he couldn't possibly see me, I was certain his diabolical words were being fed to him by the rise in my heart, because from the moment he'd started giving his speech, that same drum from our night swims, the same one from our prayer to the ocean, had begun beating inside me—and the faster it beat, the smoother my flesh became, the deeper my fever, the drunker my enthusiasm, the stronger my promise. A part of me wanted to romanticize being kidnapped and to be fucked out of my life by him. But intellectually, because I despised his sexist rebel-rapper mystique and detested the way his stupid wives shared him and catered to him, I couldn't do it.

Onstage, he was like a beautiful African lion, an actual prophet for the people. But then again, also a whore, a mama's boy, and a dictator.

"Cretin," I whispered hatefully. And just as I said it, the crowd erupted with applause, cheering him and promising to raise the signatures to place his name on the ballot for president. I looked around at the thousands gathered—poor people, overworked and underfed, draped in tattered rags—and it broke my heart to know how very desperate we are as Africans. The eyes of the people fearful and tired with an epic hope as they placed their very lives in the hands of a rap star, trusting in him to be who he said he was. Once again, since that time when our sellout kings bartered our own blood kin into slavery, African people were living at the mercy of their own black son.

"If you elect me president," Sea Horse continued as he coughed from a lung burn that he'd gotten from the marijuana smoke he held in his chest, "I make this vow, my people, that I come to equity with clean hands and that I will make West Cassavaland a development country. Death is better than disgrace . . . and I am willing to die or do whatever it takes to achieve my lifelong dream—to return honor to the African man and to restore the Twee-Sankofa Madal, the age of paradise."

The people had already begun cheering and applauding wildly.

But then Sea Horse added, "And I *promise* when I'm president that we're going to win the World Cup at least once!"

And oh my God—why did he have to say that? It became like an earthquake! The feet stomping, the screaming, the dancing, and the chanting of his name. The last time I had seen Africans so excited was the day Orisha was stomped to death, and because of that I couldn't get the holy ghost, and it seemed that the heat of the moon bore down against me—an omen of bad luck. But I wasn't listening to my intuition.

"My people!" Sea Horse called out to quiet them. "Let's not forget the offering, the ancient ways of our ancestors, the ritual from paradise days when a dark young virgin would be plucked from the masses and offered up to the king!" I couldn't believe his words, but immediately there were several women raising their hands and screaming that they should be the offerings. And then a spotlight moved toward where I stood next to Tiberius.

"I've asked for a special lady tonight . . ."

The light was so blinding I had to put my hands over my eyes. People were screaming, clapping, and chanting the word "Blacka!" (lady who the moon has chosen), and all of that would have been just fine. But it turned very ugly when my brother Tiberius reached over and began ripping my gown off, painfully tearing the fabric from my body as he shouted like a religious fanatic, "My sister is the offering!"

Then, as I fought, kicking and screaming at the pure shock of being butt naked in front of ten thousand strangers, he lifted me up—and it became *everybody* lifting me up, a mass hysteria, screaming and shaking the earth, hands and palms and fingers and more hands passing me over a sea of nappy heads until all I could do was clamp my eyes shut and pray to wake up.

But I didn't wake up. I was crying, terrified, revisited by the memories of Orisha, peeing on people's heads while I tried to fight back. African drums beat as though they were emanating from the center of the earth, and one woman hollered out to me, "Do eeeet for yah ann-cesstas!"

The ocean of hands levitated my naked body against the sky and moon, passing me from one wave in the crowd to the next, rolling me forward until I reached the stage—at which point their excitement reached fever pitch, their screams deafening, and Sea Horse smiled down on me as his guards fetched me from the arm-stilts of the mob and placed my cowering body onstage in front of him, the two of us immersed in white light, with me trying to cover everything up.

"You're the offering!" one of the topless Oluchi women shouted, and she pried my hands from between my legs with a bamboo pole. "Don't cover yourself!"

I felt so humiliated, as though I were a slave and Sea Horse was King Kong, but the people only cheered with unbridled delight while I stood there crying, fuming at the wild masculine bravado of Sea Horse's stare. I realized that even when black people endeavor to rise up Africa and restore it to paradise, there remains this thirst to debase its mother—which is what keeps Africa from rising.

"We're only going to dance and be patriotic for the crowd," Sea Horse whispered to me.

"Fuck you," I replied.

His wife Tasso, sensing that I would not be made to behave as a woman from paradise days, eased up to me from behind, embracing my nakedness, and said in my ear, sensuously, "In the dance of the water-fly, the drummer is underwater . . . *and cannot see.*"

A witch doctor danced up to Sea Horse and me as though he'd come to marry us. He handed Sea Horse a gob of chain-link and then snatched my arm upward, giving my wrist to Sea Horse to be chained—the crowd went crazy, screaming and dancing to the drumbeat of my debasement.

"He's not going to hurt you," Tasso whispered in my ear as she continued to hold me from behind.

For a moment, I resigned myself to remaining calm, but then, while lusting and appraising the silvery rich contours of my naked flesh, Sea Horse said to me, "A black woman's body isn't built for conservatism."

To which I slapped him hard with my free hand.

After I did that, the whole jungle became so quiet you could hear the trout pissing at the bottom of Lake Mona Lisa.

EXPENSIVE SHIT

Every room in Sea Horse's estate flowed into the next like an airy maze of red-tiled adobe copper-tone bunga-low suites—the sponge walls accentuated by trickling fountains, lush gardens, and panoramic baby-blue skies that blessed the top of your head as you passed below the sunroofs of certain rooms and hallways.

I refused to stay unless Tiberius slept in the same room with me for protection (leaving his wife Chiamaka with their room all to herself), though I don't know why I trusted him. We slept, hugged tight, front to front. But after the unexpected fun of being there the first two days, I decided to luxuriate in the vacation-like atmosphere and accept the fact that Sea Horse and I weren't going to be satisfied until we'd gotten the holy ghost out of our systems.

We had that stupid thing—chemistry—between us. And no matter how often I glanced at the engagement ring on my finger, I knew that James Lord didn't love me and that he'd never been faithful to me. I really didn't have a man. In some ways, the more successful my modeling career had become, the more I didn't want one. I had money, planetary freedom, and fame, so it followed that good sex alone could be an adequate stress releaser, or at least that's what I was telling myself.

"You didn't have to slap me so hard," Sea Horse laughed on the third morning as he stood over the patio grill making breakfast for everyone—egg stew, trout, yam, plantains, and white bread fried in cinnamon and butter.

I rolled my eyes, glad that he could joke about it. But I kept my stare trained on the rock-lined swimming pond where six of his children by Tasso were frolicking. The sight unsettled me, because the white wife in London had a son by him and the black American wife, Valencia, had a son and daughter in Miami.

"So tell me, mermaid—when?"

"When what?"

"When did you realize you were falling in love with the king?"

I rolled my eyes again, but also turned my head around so he wouldn't see me grinning. Then during breakfast we became like children, unable to stop smiling, chuckling, and flashing the whites of our eyes at each other, much to the delight of Tiberius and Chiamaka. But not Tasso, who ate her breakfast pondside with her children and, in front of everyone, painfully pretended that she didn't have a problem with my being there.

I had gone to Tasso several times and insisted on leaving, but she'd forbidden it, grabbing me by the shoulders and pleading, "If you leave, it will only make me look bad in front of Sea Horse."

"But your husband plans to fuck me, Tasso—and I'm attracted to him too. It's like we have to do it."

"You aren't the first and you won't be the last," she'd said with a low, heartbroken giggle. "He brings Millicent and Valencia and their children here for vacations as well. I clean up behind them too. They're just not as nice about it as you are."

"You're so young and beautiful—why do you stay?"

"I'm a Cassava wife with eight children. Where am I going to go? And besides, the love between me and Sea Horse blossomed while we were teenagers and then died with the birth of our first child. My commitment is no longer to Sea Horse, but to Allah and my culture. I am an African wife. My husband and I were born in the same village and given to each other by the elders—till death do us part. As usual, this bond means *everything* to the African woman . . . and absolutely nothing to the African man. You're an African girl, Eternity. You've seen this all your life, everywhere. Sea Horse is a gifted musician, a wonderful father, and a devoted leader for our people's causes. But when it comes to the fate of the female, he's just like any other black man—selfish. It's not going to help me for you to up and walk out—especially since I was the one who asked him to bring you here."

"What?"

"Yes," she nodded. "After he recorded the song about you and kept talking about you, I told him that his next wife had better be African or the ancestors would wreak havoc with his political ambitions. I told him he'd better find an Ajowan girl who knows how to pray to the ocean."

"Sea Horse intends to marry me?"

"Don't say it like that, and don't reject him," Tasso begged tearfully. "Let him possess you, and let us claim as much of him for Africa as we can. The white woman and that black American Akata bitch are driving his seed to complete corruption—these people are like a disease infiltrating our blood."

"I promise I'll stay a few days, Tasso. But I can tell you right now that I would never marry Sea Horse under any circumstances. I would rather go through life as a whore, free and on my own, than be walked on like a pair of sandals clinging to the bottom of a man's feet."

Tasso gently placed her hand against my face and cried, pathetically, "Don't hate our men, chei!"

DON'T HATE OUR MEN

My son: Sea Horse argued with us over breakfast, demanding, "What child wants to know the personal details of his mother's life?"

"But women are not just mothers," Chiamaka countered. Her usually childlike face took on a startling se-
riousness as Tiberius redid one of her cornrows that
had come loose. "They're human beings. No woman can
be only a whore or a saint, or just dumb or just smart.
Women are complex people."

"Kamit-Ama was a whore, nothing more!" Sea Horse
decreed in reference to the mythical Cassavan witch
who'd breastfed her warrior sons until they were nearly
twenty years old, which in turn, according to the leg-
end, brought about homosexuality. Kamit-Ama's mythical boys sprouted breasts and had to have them cut off
before they could join the other men in battle. But then
even with their breasts cut off, the boys had seduced
their fellow warriors during secluded forays in foreign
lands, contaminating the army, Sea Horse said, with gay
sex orgies, and had to be hunted down and put to death
by our nation's great warrior father, Twee Obatala.

"This is why we can't have feminism and we can't
tolerate the European faggot virus," Tiberius chimed in,
bitterly ignoring my previous announcement that I considered myself a feminist, and that I knew and loved
several gay people.

But of course it's the men who have traditionally
been the architects of paradise, and the ones who decide
what exactly makes it a paradise. All through breakfast,
Chiamaka and I sat listening as Sea Horse and Tiberius
enchanted us with epic stories (fairy tales?) about powerful ancient kingdoms where black men were smelt-
ing and working with iron eons before the Europeans
stopped dwelling in caves. Of course, as always, they
recounted the great love stories that our ancestors had

handed down from generation to generation—tales of handsome rogue warriors invading the ancient all-female villages of Kamit-Ama and other witches, duly kidnapping the ebony-skinned princess virgins, and romancing them until their satiny black wombs filled up the continent with strong dark sons.

"Twee Obatala had no choice but to slay Kamit-Ama. Her silly goddess religion went against nature."

"That's according to the *men's* history!" Chiamaka retorted with a pout.

"The history of the African man is the history of all Africans," Tiberius responded to his wife. "Sisters don't need a separate history book. We're already telling your story!"

Chiamaka and I were preparing to refute him when Tasso came over to clear away our empty breakfast dishes and wipe the table down. Out of respect for the men, she spoke without making eye contact with anyone at the table. Her huge fig-shaped lips admonished us: "A woman is a flower in a garden—her husband the fence around it."

"Enshalla," Sea Horse clapped to the African proverb that every West African child grows up with.

Tasso continued: "A cow, a donkey, a sheep, a goat, a *wife*—it is at five that a man succeeds."

Sea Horse and Tiberius laughed, slapping their thighs as Chiamaka rolled her eyes with contempt.

Then Tasso, wide of hip and always angelic-looking in her flowing satin burka, lowered the boom by saying, "Forgive these foolish modern black women who've forgotten their place beside the black man. Just as our ancestors told us—a woman cannot see her palm. They have forgotten the natural order of things, that to beget woman is to beget man. That the man dies in the road and the woman dies in the house."

A woman cannot see her palm.

Suddenly, I remembered the dolls lined up on the ground. Ma Nonni's hand guiding mines as I resisted, but her voice insisting, "Heaven is the cut between an African woman's legs."

Bare-breasted black women with baskets atop their heads sang: "A cow, a donkey, a sheep, a goat, a wife, pleasure be the man's life . . . pleasure be the man's life . . . pleasure be the man's life."

She was cutting the doll's imaginary vagina with her hand over mines. "Practice makes perfect, Orisha—you must learn wrist control, or you'll kill somebody's child." Then, with my sister's hand, Ma Nonni was teaching us how to make the cuts local families paid her to make on their own rows of young daughters.

"You must remove the worm of pleasure from between the little girl's legs."

"No, Ma . . . please, no!"

"The African woman is treasured for her obedience, her soulful beauty, her wide hips to bring sons, her strong back to carry kings, her voice to raise up the ocean in song. The African woman is but a flower in a garden—her husband the fence around it."

Eternity?

Yoo-hoo, Eternity?

Blinking, I caught my breath, but not before a dozen diamond-sized tears tripped over my bottom eyelids, my mouth quivering as I tried not to cry.

"Are you OKAY?"

And when an alarmed Tiberius put his hand on my shoulder in support, I wept quietly, remembering the gnarled flesh between Orisha's legs and told God, "I hate dolls."

THE NATURAL MAN HAS MANY WOMEN

Will Sea Horse be disappointed that I'm not circumcised?

I wondered about that, and especially because he claimed to be Muslim—although, in all fairness to the Muslim people, I have to say that he and Tasso were the most unorthodox Muslims I'd ever met (they were more like river people). But then again, Sea Horse did make it a point to pray five times a day facing Mecca and often greeted people with, "As-salaam alaikum."

"Come," Tasso said to me one afternoon while carrying a huge platter of marijuana that she'd washed, dried, and baked and was about to chop and roll into fat white cigarettes for Sea Horse. "You can help me prepare Big Papa's smokes for the week, and this way you'll learn how he likes things done."

Big Papa? It had taken everything in me not to crack up laughing in Tasso's face. But I contained myself and helped out. Her elegant rolling of the weed in delicate white tissues and then the tip of her tongue cat-licking it into a blunt didn't seem to go with her rich woman's burka, but nonetheless Tasso accomplished it expertly. She informed me, "Sea Horse is taking you to London next week. He's nominated for the British Galaxy Music Award, and he wants you to watch him win."

I can't be photographed in public with Sea Horse Twee—I'm engaged to marry James Lord! And of all places, London. The press will have a field day giving me the same black eye they give Naomi Campbell.

Tasso was trying to warn me about something, but I was distracted and hadn't caught on yet. There was an undercurrent of polite hostility as she said, "And while you're in London, Sea Horse wants to make love to you in an environment where no one from the press can spy on you. So . . . you'll be staying at the cobblestone walk-up that he keeps for Millicent York and her child Garvey. This means that Millicent has to leave her home so that Sea Horse can romance you in London."

"I can't go to London with Sea Horse."

"Well, Millicent is extremely upset," Tasso whispered. "She's threatening divorce over this. What's worse is that she'll be here tomorrow. Sea Horse is making her bring Garvey to Africa."

The next afternoon, when Millicent swept into the compound with her pale, chalky complexion draped in a colorful West African tunic with traditional gele and cowry shells, it was impossible not to stare. She had the look that white women can't shake in Africa—that of being unnaturally out of place to the African eye, bringing clarity to Sea Horse's saying, *We who go with the landscape*.

"Millicent York, this is Eternity Franken—"

"I know who she is. She was cavorting with Sea Horse at the resort last season. Hello, dear. You're a full black one, aren't ye?"

Up close in the face, Millicent reminded me of tough white girls who worked in canning factories. Though she'd been very skinny when Sea Horse first met her, she was now thick and box-shaped with a wide, flat ass and traveled everywhere with a pack of macaroons in her purse. Her white flesh kept her from being accused of having a bad attitude, but there was a permanent scowl on her face. The more you stared into her hazel-gray eyes, the more you could see that she counted as one of her only victories in life her stature over black people in their own communities.

"She's very bitter because she thinks I ruined her life," Sea Horse would tell me months later. "She comes from a notable family in England, but out of their three daughters, she was the one who had to be smart to get attention. She was a feminist writing against the sexism in rap music when I met her; very angry at her father. I don't lie about it—I was barely a teenager with a huge hit in the UK, and all I did in England was put my tree branch up in white girls. I thought I'd gone to heaven, you know? Me, this nap-haired dang-boy from Cassava-land being chased and put on a pedestal by the daughters of the colonial white boss father! *Great Christ, the fuck!* I thought every one of them looked like a goddess, because you know how white women are—they just have that mystique, that running-horse beauty; they look just like the women you see on television or in movies, just valuable, you know? And besides, my ma always wanted a Fanta baby. You know this type of African lady, the ones in the cities who wear wigs. Well, that's my ma. She swallowed arsenic wafers and kept her skin rubbed down in Nadinola skin-bleaching cream because she believed that God loves light-skinned people more. So I did it with my ma in mind. Tried to get five or six of those white girls to marry me, the prettiest ones, but I didn't have the money then like I have it now—and if they were going to marry black, they'd rather marry a black American celebrity, because he's the richest kind

of black and he's already a member of the European culture. But Millicent was different from the pretty white
girls. She wasn't interested in money. She loved me for
me and was fascinated by my music and my culture—
she started writing articles in the British press about
slavery in Sudan, debt relief, racial injustice in Brixton,
and the white race's evil against African people. She said
she wanted to escape being seen as a white woman, because that's not what she is—she's a human being—and
love knows no color, no race between individuals. And
really, Eternity, that's what we were by the time I got
over my phase of idolizing white skin and long hair—
two individuals in love."

In his eyes, I could see it was true. That what he and
Millicent had stumbled into was genuine love. But then
Sea Horse said, "Things changed when Garvey came.
If he'd been a girl, it would have been different—but
that type of hair on a boy, it's not African. It scared me
that this white woman could dominate my African seed.
That's why I named him after Marcus Garvey. I know it's
silly, but I don't like his hair. Garvey not having African
hair makes me feel like he's not mines. That's when our
love started to die. Millicent's a smart woman and she
picked up on my coolness toward Garvey. Luckily, my
ma idolized him. He was the child she'd always wanted to
have herself—bright orange skin with curly Been-to hair.
My ma helped a lot, because Millicent's family wasn't
too thrilled to see Garvey. I mean, they were always polite, never racist or anything—not necessarily against
us, but just not *interested* in us. And that's how they treat
Garvey, like they're not interested. It causes Millicent
to be angry and resentful all the time. Mad at me, her

family, Africa, the whole world. She expects society to just accept her interracial relationship as normal. But beyond the surface political correctness, ain't nobody trying to love no feminist white chick with a black baby, chei. Plus, with all that, there are moments when you can tell she wishes she never had Garvey, like she just wants to run away or something. Like I said, I wish she never had him too. She hates me for wishing that—so we're always mad at each other."

In front of me, however, Millicent never acted angry toward Sea Horse. Instead, she worked overtime to laugh, preen, share inside jokes via ricocheting eye contact, and be as fresh in her affection and ownership as possible. She spoke in Sea Horse's language, then looked at me like I should be impressed. When he wasn't around, she lectured Chiamaka and me on the importance of feminism and claimed "sisterhood." I shrugged at the thought. In fact, I mostly ignored her. My goal was to fuck Millicent's husband, not take him. I had nothing against her personally.

Several hours after Millicent York's arrival that day, when I saw Tasso kneeling in front of her on the living room floor like some slave, her girlish black hands vigorously massaging the fish-belly white feet of this frothy European, I realized that I was prejudiced—that save for my mother, I despised white women. Not because of their cultural tourism or their great boundless luck with the hearts of African men, but for their unfair position in the world—for being considered "the virtuous part of the Bible." The white man's mother: the superior womb of earth, imbuing humanity with whiteness and light; awarded privilege, respect, and freedom; valued and loved by sheer genetic caveat and by the utter echo of her white son's world domination. And yet standing in the doorway, what I felt for Tasso as I studied her washing and rubbing Millicent's feet was ten times worse than what I could ever feel about a white woman. Knelt down before some white bitch like a slave, I hated her.

PASSPORT

"I want you to come with me to my mother's clinic and have an AIDS test performed, Sea Horse. Dr. Juliet's results are the only ones I can trust. We won't tell her who you are—you'll be completely anonymous—but we must get tested."

ERASURE

On the plane to London, Sea Horse carefully choreographed the way in which we would first make love. He explained that it was very important to him that he fuck me right after he'd swept the British Galaxy Music Awards. I had refused to be photographed with him in public while in London, and forbade him from revaling to the media that the song "One Night Angel" was about me, so we agreed that he would attend the award ceremony with his usual entourage of bad boys while I waited at his secluded cobblestone town house, draped across Millicent's bed in sexy lingerie he would pick out for me.

"I get a trophy for writing the song," he explained while tenderly nibbling my ear, "then I get to come home and finally make love to the girl I wrote it about."

While outlining my lips with a single finger, he asked if I suck dick and swallow, and I demurely nodded.

He whispered in my ear: "Can I lick your asshole?"

Embarrassed by such a question, I shook my head.

When some horribly violent fate is just about to befall an animal in the wild, it runs for the high ground—leaving the area where death is about to enter. But having died and been brought back to life only to realize that the world was even more fucked up than when I'd left it, I found myself desensitized to my intuition; and knowing there's no such thing as death, I no longer feared it or expected it.

"Tasso likes calling me *Master*. She likes to be slapped around when I fuck her—and Millicent likes me to spit in her face at the moment when I cum."

"I sleep with my panties down," I told him.

Sea Horse made me touch it, pulling my fingers toward the bulge in his pants leg until I could make out the hardened shape of his beer-can cock. With his free hand, he fondled one of my breasts through my blouse, plucking and teasing the nipple until some internal rain mist wet up the rose between my legs and made me throw back my head, trying to arrest and control the ecstasy.

The day of the awards ceremony, London was covered with rain. Sea Horse still went out and shopped for the lingerie he wanted me to wear that evening, but by the time he returned, he had to head right back out to the show. There were press junkets and parties to attend, and when you counted the four-hour ceremony and all the preevents leading up to the broadcast, it stood that Sea Horse would be gone at least twelve hours. So I decided to entertain myself by donning large sunglasses and a floppy hat and taking a cab to the Thames Cumberland Museum to see an exhibition of the latest works from black American sculptor Decco Douglass. In particular, I was dying to see his newest piece, which was a cloth painting of West Cassavaland's legendary fire witch, Kamit-Ama.

The baroque-styled jazz of Thelonious Monk floated in the hall as my short heels click-clacked around the parquet floors, my eyes searching aimlessly for this grand salute to my countrywoman or myth or whatever she was. I glanced over and realized that the oblong image attached over a plate of baobab wood was supposed to be the rendering of her.

Slowly, I walked over to behold Kamit-Ama, this deity of both good and evil that we Cassavans speak and sing about as much as we do Twee Obatala and Ajowa, goddess of the sea—but the woman depicted looked nothing like an Oluchi goddess. The black American artist had muted the facial features, slenderizing the nose and removing the West African lazy brow that I'd been told to look for all my life. He had given Kamit-Ama the most absurd yellowish-brown complexion and long, masculine plaited hair. Her breasts, which would have surely been exposed to the sun, were covered with cowrie shells, the shape of her eyes European, and only her ears were accurate—the stretched lobes flowing past her shoulders. Tragically, the sculpture failed to honor the Kamit-Ama that our elders and griots had passed down. Once again, I felt the same crippling feelings of erasure that I'd experienced when *The Racist* premiered with a half-caste girl in the role of Orisha.

I floated back to the movie house where the African audience had thrown bottles at the screen, chanting, "*Without our real mother . . . we cannot be born!*"

Why? I wondered. Why couldn't they show an African woman as both beautiful and fully black as she is in real life? And why couldn't they ever show a movie that featured a pure-black man in love with a pure-black woman? Why is that taboo even for the eyes of the biracial? Why not celebrate black people's wholeness, instead of glorifying images of fully white men in love with fully white women as the height of normalcy?

I sickened as I reached conclusions about how systemic and diabolically planned the division was between black humans and real power. Just as I was about to turn and leave, a twenty-something guy from my country walked up, holding hands with his white girlfriend. He said of the portrait, "Isn't she beautiful? She makes me proud to be a Cassavan."

The girlfriend chirped, "Remember that movie we saw, *The Racist*? This sort of reminds me of her."

Before I could catch myself, I'd invaded their space, hissing at the boyfriend, "That's not what Kamit-Ama looked like! Don't you even remember what your mothers and sisters and aunts look like? How can you call yourself African? And that watered-down bitch in *The Racist* doesn't look a goddamned thing like Orisha—*I am Orisha*! Don't you see what's going on here?"

They stared at me like I was crazy. It suddenly dawned on me that he *wanted* his mother and sisters and aunts to look like this—because society kept insisting this is what they *should* look like. And since he obviously didn't care enough about the Cassavan women he'd been raised and nurtured by to defend them, I hated the ground he stood on. As usual, he probably thought my reaction was because he had a white girlfriend, fucking typical Pogo-nigger.

Then, right before I could run away full of self-righteous indignation over the world's colorist eye, his white girlfriend burst my bubble: "Aren't you Eternity, the famous supermodel? Can I have your autograph? Your face is on every billboard in London!"

WOMAN IS, MAN DOES

As I lay strewn across Millicent's bed in the negligee Sea Horse had picked out for me, the last thing I wanted in my state of depression was to be sexed by a black man. But I'd already promised to be the evening's second prize.

Around midnight, Sea Horse dragged himself into the bedroom, sulking and sighing. "Did you watch the show?" he asked.

"No, I taped it," I replied groggily, forcing myself into a sexy pose along the edge of the bed. But the last thing on Sea Horse's mind was sex. Africa's foremost recording star hadn't won a single British Galaxy Award.

"This is just fucked up!" he raged, then flung a wine glass into the mirror, cracking it badly. "That fucking Lucky Dube!"

Of course, Lucky Dube was a huge South African reggae star. He'd won both the Afrobeat Album of the Year and Best African Male awards while Rokia Traoré of Mali had stolen Best African Song, Best Dance Track, and Concert Performer of the Year.

"I'm a fucking genius!" Sea Horse bellowed indignantly. "How could I not get one fucking award? My albums outsell everybody's, but critics hold it against me that I don't rap in pidgin!"

I wanted to calm him down, but I was afraid.

"Rub my back, mermaid!" he ordered.

Pulling his shirt over his head after he'd sat on the edge of the bed, I sunk my fingers into the heat of his back and began massaging his muscles as therapeutically as I could. His hurt was so deep that he did something that I couldn't in a million years have imagined him doing—he wept.

"I'm never good enough, no matter what I do!" he lamented.

I knew enough to protect his pride by pretending not to notice he was crying. I said from behind his back, "You are just too much, Sea Horse. You're going to make such a wonderful leader. I can't wait, *Mr. President.*"

"But you can't stand me!" The truth in his accusation sent chills down my spine, because before that moment I hadn't realized such a thing. "You hate me."

"No," I said unconvincingly.

"*Yes.* You hate me. Deep inside, all black people hate each other—don't you know that?"

"No," I stumbled. "Some white people cloned me. I don't know anything."

Sea Horse laughed as I now lost my composure. I had my face buried in my hands as he said, "Well, that's a good one, because it's the only way to describe Africa. We speak English, French, Arabic, and its slave language, Swahili—it's like *Invasion of the Body Snatchers*, chei. The whole fucking continent is a clone." He pulled my hands away from my tear-stained face and asked, "Now that we've hated, do you think we could be in love?"

To which I replied, honestly, "Woman is, man does."

But Sea Horse didn't get it. He said, "The natural man has many women, and if you could stop holding that against me and accept it, I could make you my queen. Not a mere wife like Tasso, Valencia, and Millicent, but my African Queen, my true love."

"I'm already my own queen, Sea Horse—with or without you."

Gracefully and with the most surprising tenderness, he cupped one of my breasts with his hand and lightly squeezed and bobbed it before devouring it with his mouth. His tongue aroused the nipple as he sucked and shaped the tit, masterfully, into a kind of human fruit. He then pulled away, his eyes spying mines for some glint of thought, and began to sing, "I know a girl so black . . . she doesn't need clothes. I tried to find where I left her . . . but nobody knows."

For the first time in all my lives, I felt as though I were getting to the good part.

Sea Horse surprised me with it—deep and soft and sudden. His sincerity tasted like water from a clear spring; the gentle caress of his hands felt like breezes that he'd gathered up from night walks by the sea and saved just for this moment.

I know I sound foolish, but it felt so good being a fool.

It was as though I'd lived every moment just to get to this one. Our first kiss, I swear to you, was so illicit and so meant to be that I couldn't believe we'd never kissed before. I felt the goodness of his heart, and tasted the raindrops in his dream world, and I liked it.

Sea Horse said to me, "I can wait until you're ready."

"A woman is never ready," I laughed back at him. Then, all too soon, he was asleep—gently snoring on the pillow like some prized lion, his body crouched against mines (an African man from the city!). I still hadn't been penetrated by Sea Horse—and still didn't know if I wanted to be.

OTHERS

Tangled on the bed, we were sleeping deeply when the most hideous telephone call came. It was my agent saying he'd just gotten off African Airlines flight 457 from Senegal and had been served by a stewardess who he insisted was me—not just a girl with an uncanny resemblance, not a look-alike, but quite literally me. He was extremely shaken up by this.

I felt like throwing up. My worst fear was a reality: Stevedore and Dr. Juliet had cloned other Eternities in secret. I wondered if my mother had even cloned Hope.

I couldn't sleep for the rest of that night, and confronted my mother over the telephone first thing in the morning: "You sick, twisted bitch—you fucking bitch! You can't clone people and play God and—"

"You're being paranoid, Eternity. Nothing of the sort is going on."

REMEMBERING ANDY WARHOL

Sea Horse and I flew to America on separate flights, hoping to keep our secret flame under wraps in New York City. Out of nowhere, while Sea Horse was busy appearing on MTV and raising foreign interest for his presidential bid, the avant-garde American movie director Quentin Q. convinced me to appear in his new movie, *The Film About Andy Warhol*.

I was to appear in a cameo as iconic 1970s singer, model, and actress Grace Jones, a close friend and muse of Warhol's. I couldn't imagine it—my soft and feminine temperament was very girlish in comparison to the photos and footage he showed me of Jones—but Quentin was convinced that with my strong bone structure, he could make me into her. After a full day of rehearsal, I shot my two scenes with a husky voice and wore a slinky-sexy outfit.

I returned to our hotel in Manhattan that evening and listened to the sounds of this enchanting American stylist, Dionne Warwick. I relaxed on the terrace and sipped wine as I floated on the wings of her amazing 1960s bossa nova songs.

Sea Horse soon returned and made me dance to long steamy remixes of "Mombassa" and D'banj's "Tongolo." He tried to use contagious laughter to set the mood for our lovemaking, but I felt frigid and distracted. I was fighting against falling in love with him.

He whispered in my ear, "Being in a film means you're immortal now."

I know what that word means, and it's awful.

GET DE FUCK OUT

With the news that Sea Horse's name had been successfully added to the presidential election ballot came violence.

Sea Horse and I had decided to chance it and return home on the same flight. In fact, I was still on the plane after landing back in DakCrete when gunmen fired on him. Sea Horse and his bodyguards had exited the air-craft and were heading down the staircase when I heard the shout, "Get de fuck out!"

Then gunshots: *POP! POP! POP!*

Peeking out the passenger window, I glimpsed the shooters' raggedy jeep speeding away.

"Mama!" Sea Horse was calling, painfully. "Ma!"

I ran down to him, stopping in my tracks where his body and those of his bodyguards blocked the narrow steps. There was blood splattered everywhere, but I could tell they were all alive. Emergency personnel from inside the airport were racing to the scene.

"Don't move," I said to Sea Horse. "You're badly hurt."

"*Mer*-maid," he mumbled in a blur before going unconscious.

As he was put on a stretcher and lifted into an am-bulance, I was too distraught to care about the cameras click-clicking photographs of supermodel Eternity Fran-kenheimer crying, kissing, and clinging to Sea Horse's hand.

"I have to go with him!" I screamed at the paramed-ics. "I'm his *wife!*" I lied.

And whoever was lucky enough to be there with a camera that day made himself a pretty penny, because before nightfall the photos of me attending to Sea Horse's assassination attempt were all over the television and

Internet, and, by the next day, all over the front pages of the major European, Australian, Middle Eastern, and African newspapers.

The Earth Has Parents

O f the three of them, I still haven't figured out which of my men is your father. With skin my color, the daddy could be the whitest penguin from the North Pole and the baby would still come out pure chocolate. But one thing I can honestly say is that I loved all my men with all my heart. Not in the same ways or for the same reasons or even with the same intensity, but I found out that nothing was more important to me than to love and to be loved in return. And, since none of the men in this new journey had actually been offering me what most people would consider "true love," I was forced to take what I could get, which is usually how a woman ends up with more than one man in the first place.

Do you understand what I'm telling you?

Water Lily Coffee

I slipped into the room, quietly crying, as I'd just broken up with James Lord over the phone and had thrown his ring away. Sea Horse lay asleep, his chest and leg bandaged, with a pan of water lilies on the table next to him and another beneath his bed.

Root Magic

"Water lilies are not used as table food by Europeans and Americans," Tasso explained as I assisted her in preparing a traditional spiritual recipe for Sea Horse. "Only people of color—we are the ones who know about the special power of water lilies and how delicious they are. You pay attention to what I'm teaching you now, sister."

As requested, I brought fresh brown eggs to her—no white ones. Tasso cracked four of them into a bowl of waakye (red beans and rice), then squished together the yokes and waakye with cous cous using her bare black fingers.

"Brown eggs are good for the brain—white eggs are bad for the heart," she instructed. "When outsiders plot to kill your son, a mother remembers that the earth has parents. Nothing is above her; she is the black mother. Let me see the protein."

I lifted the pale of crayfish that Tiberius, Chiamaka, and I had netted from the river, but first they had to be seasoned the Cassavan way. Tasso boiled several ears of corn, then added the live crayfish, stirring them with a wooden spoon until their shells became a brilliant red.

"Hand me the water lilies."

Lightly flicking palm oil on them with her fingertips, she spooned the fufu and waakye egg mixture into the leaves, rolling them up on a cookie sheet as one would stuff cabbage leaves before sliding them into the oven. She then brought out a loaf of bread into which she'd baked the seeds from the lilies.

"For the spell to work," Tasso continued, "it is crucial that we mix a teaspoon of the chopped root of the water lilies with a teaspoon of each of these herbs."

I watched as she combined the chopped lily root in a cup with the two most important of the herb blends: geech (burdock root and red clover) and sula (common rue). She then added red bush (Rooibos), chervil, the shavings of white willow bark, pulse cassia (legume), and kola nut, then topped the mixture with the aniseed-flavored herb, sweet cicely.

"Hand me the blood."

The bowl of "blood" was actually a poor people's coffee the villagers made from the roasted seeds of white water lilies colored with red palm oil. Before mixing the blood with the magical herbs, many of which taste unpleasant, Tasso whipped up a delicious spicy sauce by adding into the red coffee a cup of fresh honey, spicy red pepper, musa (sweet bananas that have been fried, mashed, dried, and shaved to a powder), trout stock, and tamarind. Out of the tubers (the delicious potato of the water lily, which can be eaten raw or cooked), Tasso made sliced cheese wafers.

"I want you to take it up to him, Eternity. Go to him respectfully—barefoot, and keep your head bowed. Do not look at him, and do not speak unless spoken to."

Old Ways

I took the tray to Sea Horse's room. He smiled broadly when he saw me enter with it. After I set it up in front of him, I leaned down and kissed him on the forehead, much like a young girl kisses her father.

"They want to kill me . . . to stop our people's revolution."

Kill Switch

The U.S. State Department called them the "African mafia." Of these two notorious killers, one was a makeshift Christian, the other a makeshift Muslim. Sea Horse stood on his porch, his muscular chest bandaged elaborately, and stared down into the men's faces.

"Ya steel gawn run for prez-ah-deeent, baby boy?" one of them asked.

Tiberius stood directly behind Sea Horse with a sawed-off shotgun. You could see it in his face that he disapproved of Sea Horse calling in the mafia, but here was life.

Against an orange sky, their dust-covered black Mercedes resembled a license-plated vulture awaiting the death of a starving infant. Chiamaka nervously served them chunky wedges of watermelon as I leaned against a tree staring at Sea Horse's Adam's apple, the boldness of his throat, the tenseness of his jaws.

"Your story is all over de world media," said the tall, skinny Oluchi Muslim wearing a suit and dark glasses.

The fat Christian one added, "De world community is outraged at these kind of political scare tactics. Just like what Bush is doing in Iraq right now—people don't like it. But it don mean shit, boy. America and Europe still pud dey money behind Yaw Ibrahim. You got no sponsor."

"I need protection," Sea Horse admitted. "An army of black fuckers wid guns 'n shit, man. I'm going for the presidency."

"You want a money deal with the Arabs?"

"But Arabs are backing Yaw Ibrahim!" Tiberius chimed in.

"No, no, some different Arabs. These ones would need you to promote Islam in the villages, teach West Africans Arabic instead of English. Bring the poor people discipline," the Muslim said. "Ibrahim's got his white man, and you need your white man—you can't be a president of Africa without de white man."

"I can't roll wid the oil militias. I'm against sharing oil!"

"How about the Chinese den? The Chinese need a good boy in Africa even more den de white man does."

"I'm not ruling as no Pogo-nigger, chei!"

"You have to rule as a Pogo-nigger, baby boy. What, you think you're Mugabe? You want to end up dead like Lumumba or Steven Biko, or would you rather retire someday in peace, like Obanjo, to de chicken ranch?"

The Christian said, "Chinese is a hard language to learn, but they don't force their religion on you like de white and de Arab. They let you make up your own prayers."

THE CROWN

On the night that all eleven of Sea Horse's children were gathered around his bed to hear the single most important fable in African history—"The Story of the Crown"—Tasso insisted that I be present in the row of wives. I already felt uneasy in the presence of Sea Horse's mother, Ma Binata, who had been disgusted by my pitch-black coloring from the moment she laid eyes on me, saying, "You're too black to be a good person." The funny thing was, she wasn't too far from the same color herself.

As we gathered behind the children in Sea Horse's bedroom, all ears ready to take in his bedtime story, I smiled sweetly at Ma Binata's synthetic wig-wearing, squat, tugboat self, watching as she nestled close to

Sea Horse's black American wife, Valencia, who she did adore because she didn't look anything like a black woman. Valencia possessed sparkling violet eyes, skin lighter than yoke custard, and long, fluffy dark hair. She looked Hawaiian. Her children by Sea Horse were pretty—tall and brown toast–colored with clean, even features.

"Come to Nana," Ma Binata cheered affectionately as her favorite grandchild, Garvey, who I also considered to be the sweetest of the children, entered the room with Millicent. Ma Binata immediately nudged Valencia out of the way to sweep up Garvey in her flabby black arms, pecking him with kisses and flashing her eyes approvingly at his white mother.

"Hello, Mother Binata." Millicent reveled in the fact that her white genes and chromosomes made her the favorite daughter-in-law. (But, of course, we would learn the next day that Millicent York was filing for divorce—not because Sea Horse had taken me to London to fuck me in her bed, but because the whole world had found out about it.)

To my surprise, Garvey then handed me an African violet he had plucked from the river and said, "For my tallest mommy."

But out of all the batches of children, Tasso's were the most familiar and gorgeous to me, truly West Cassavan. And as I watched them, I understood why Tasso, the first time we met, had introduced herself as Sea Horse's "God-given wife." Not only had she and Sea Horse come from the same tribe and village, but their sons looked almost like clones of Sea Horse, while the daughters were a rich, muddy Mandingo brown with slender bodies, close-cropped hair, and faces as delicately rind-thick and enchanting as those of our Cassava ancestors.

It was also clear that all the different mixtures of children were absolutely desperate for their father's love. You could see in their eyes—that ultrabright dead retina that possesses children who feel inadequate and unloved—both loving and hating a parent until all goodness grows numb.

Out of the traditional mantra of the African royals, Sea Horse said to his daughters: "Through our children we live forever." Then to his sons: "Any man who doesn't know the history of his people perishes from the earth."

He spoke first about being a little boy in DakCrete. His father, a cab driver, was brutally beaten for filing a complaint against the government officials who he'd driven from the airport to the presidential palace after they'd refused to pay the fare. "Your grandpa died in a jail cell from internal bleeding because he was man enough to demand to be paid for his work."

Sea Horse continued: "Once upon a time, there was a great mighty warrior, the father of all your father's people—Twee Obatala. He lived in a beautiful paradise with his wife and kids. He mostly hunted and fished, smoked some herb, and made music on his drum—but then one day he was coming back from playing in the river with his family when he heard a thunderous voice call his name . . . It wasn't another man, though—it was a burning bush. And the bush said, 'Hey, I'm your creator man . . . and I made you in my image, with the crown of all knowledge on your head, and I gave you this paradise so you would always have everything you need.' So anyway—God goes on to tell Twee Obatala that there are some strange, greedy men coming to Africa to steal his land, rape his wife, kill his children, and, most of all—to remove his crown. God says to Obatala, 'No matter what they do to you, there's no way they can defeat you as long as you have the crown on your head. And I gave no other race of people this crown. Only you and those with your blood possess the one true hair, the crown of wool, the greatness of beauty that is the proof that I made you first and that you are my chosen son—my symbol of wholeness, where others split apart. So in all you do, fight the good fight, but never lose your crown. Because without it, you are no longer the chosen one.

"A true African never loses his crown," conclued Sea Horse. "It is the proof that he has not been defeated by the white man or the Arab, the Indian or the Asian. It is the proof that he is still his own man, marked separately as God's chosen son. Now come, each of you, give Papa some sugar."

TREASURE

In my sleep, he was staring down at me from a tree branch—a young, sweet little gingerbread boy with huge saucer eyes and a button nose. When I asked him what his name was, thinking that he was you, son—he said, "I'm Jesus Christ."

And then somebody tweaked my nose, causing me to jump awake!

In the dark, I couldn't really see.

"Don't scream," Sea Horse whispered.

"Why are you watching me sleep?"

"Because asleep you remind me of that story *Sleeping Beauty*—you look like somebody drew you with a steady hand."

CONNECTIVE TISSUE

It finally happened between Sea Horse and me. A kiss that felt like a boil being lanced, it was fire. I felt like a child beneath Sea Horse's wounded body, our searching, feverish mouths smack-crashing and blistering with the sweetest, most impatient embraces. And before I could process that it was actually happening, I felt the sharp stab of his penis taking potshots at the butterflies in my stomach. *Oh God!* I don't know why I'd expected it to be a different dance than the one with Stevedore and James, but it was that same animal beauty with a black man. I moaned over his shoulder, hoping that the other women in the house (the children!) couldn't hear what was happening. I opened my legs wider and gyrated my curvy hips in time with his muscled ones, our froglike metaphysics dampening the bed with sweat as his *black* dick speared faster and faster until all the spasms in my body melted like a buttery dew tranquil between my legs.

"Who dis pussy, eh?" he demanded as he sloshed in and out of me. "Who dis pussy?"

"Yours," I'd cried in ecstasy. "Yours, Sea Horse."

INTERMISSION

The following night, Sea Horse paced around his bedroom in a rage. Millicent York had served him with di-

164)(THE SEXY PART OF THE BIBLE

vorce papers and the West Cassavaland government was trying to cover its ass in the world community by scheduling him for a full hour's live interview on our nation's only broadcast network.

"You're a candidate for president, so please wear a suit and tie. The whole world will be watching," the representative from the White House had said. But Sea Horse seemed too distracted by Millicent to care.

"Fucking bitch!" he raged, incredulously. "She's doing this to get herself a white man—which is what she always wanted in the first place. That's why she's letting my mother keep Garvey. So she won't have any little darkie to explain."

On the one hand, he insisted that he was sick of Millicent York and was no longer attracted to her—which was true; you could see it in his eyes. But on the other, he had a paranoid fear that she would now go out and choose a white man as her next mate.

Because I had been raised by a white man, it came as a surprise to me that so many black men saw their lives as a big ongoing competition against white men. Later, I was stunned to realize that Sea Horse had the same insecurities I did about being "good enough" for a white mate. Everything I held in secret, it seemed like he held too. And I felt sad that neither he nor I knew love.

No Love

As the days passed, I found myself crying for no reason when I was alone. I started to get nosebleeds, and when Chiamaka and I went to DakCrete to browse the boutique windows on the boulevards, two different Cassavan passersby stared at me and said, "You need Jesus."

"It's what they say to women with charcoal skin who have the nerve to walk around the city with the rest of us," Chiamaka explained from a more acceptable chocolate-fudge vantage point.

Of course, everywhere we went that day, we saw people sporting the black armband with the red splotch in the middle that Sea Horse had worn during his national television interview to chants of, *Vote for the Motherland Party, not the Fatherland.*" And then on Ball Road, where we got yams and Fanta, Chiamaka brought me to the cart of an old gray-haired Yoruba woman.

"Lady Adeyemi, this is my friend Eternity."

"What a pretty, *pretty* black girl," the woman said, nearly singing it. She kept calling me "sey-su" (favorite daughter).

"Thank you."

"Give me your hand, sey-su," said the wrinkly woman. As if by magic, she suddenly said, "You're a dead woman brought back to life by sorcery—an actual goddess."

"Lady Adeyemi!" Chiamaka gasped.

But the Yoruba woman kept her gaze on me. "I mean what I say. This girl has been resurrected and she'll be resurrected again. Tell me, Eternity—who is this man with three nipples?"

The question turned Chiamaka to stone. "My husband," she replied quietly.

The woman then asked me, "Do you know what it means when a woman's nose bleeds around children?"

"That she's going to die or have a baby," I recited.

"Rubbish! It means that she's falling in love when

she doesn't want to. But she can't get out of it. And children are the proof that men and women can truly love. You're falling in love for the first time."

"But I've been in love before."

"No, sey-su. Not like this."

Back at the estate that evening, my agent telephoned from London to congratulate me on a new contract with Second Moon Cosmetics. On top of that, I'd been offered another acting role in a big-budget Hollywood science-fiction flick.

"I'll have to leave in a few days," I told Sea Horse when he came to my room. "I have to get back to my career."

"So what about us? . . . I want you to be my wife, Eternity."

"I can't do that, Sea Horse. You're married to too many women as it is. You've got a house full of kids."

He looked annoyed. "What do you want from a man?"

"I don't know, but I can't be part of a harem. I'm too good for that."

"Then what about Africa, black woman? It's your legacy, your heritage, to sacrifice yourself for Mother Africa."

"It is?" I asked with amusement.

"You're a black woman, a Cassavan. You should know that. Don't you remember paradise—carrying my food on your head and my seed on your back? Kneeling at my feet and fetching my water? You, black woman, would eat the nuts out of my shit if I told you to. It's not easy being a woman, but with me, it's all you'll know."

THE EARTH HAS PARENTS

I felt like Sleeping Beauty writhing at the bottom of Sea Horse's beautiful dream, body to body, our lovemaking contained by a bed of sickle fire floating through night on the backs of antelope. The part that made it wrong was the part that made it right. All his prayers, kisses, caresses, and all his hopes, fears, and truths seeped inside me until like an antibiotic they searched out and quarantined the part of me that was already him.

"Don't resist being a man, mermaid," he hummed as our bucking bodies burnt up in the fire. "You are the one raised by scientists. Half of the sea horse is a woman, never resisting wholeness. Wholeness is the roundness of the earth—the two-fold of the earth and sea, the naked love."

Rush to meet my feet, Ocean . . . Wash over me, eternally.
Let me be the shepherd of your sea, Ajowan woman.
Goddess . . . becoming more and more of herself.

I didn't want it to end, the masterfulness of his love stroke or the deepness of the dream that he was planting inside me. But out of nowhere and beyond my control, our bodies shook like an earthquake, my hand atrophied like a seashell pressed against his lava-hot chest, and the roaring wind song of all seven seas—the sweetest sound I've ever made, son—swept us back into the real world. As his penis went limp and I tasted the salt of his sweat glazing over me, Sea Horse sucked a drag of his marijuana cigarette and whispered, tenderly, "This is why people stay mad at God . . . too much life and not enough lovemaking."

STAY

I've heard that in America, the black people have a saying, "Stay black and die." It fascinates me, because in Africa we have the same saying, only it goes, "Stay black and *live*."

Stay black and live.

My baby brother had been pumping his fist in the air and chanting those words when they killed him.

I found out about Tiberius by phone.

"Eternity—it's Tasso. Are you sitting down, dearest one?"

A mob of swallowers and skin bleachers had gathered around Tiberius on the streets of DakCrete, brandishing bottles and tire irons. They wanted the boxes of pills in the raggedy Chevrolet station wagon to be set free, and were prepared to move him by any means necessary. But they'd arrived to find a half-caste, biracial protestor—the very vision of what they themselves dreamt of becoming.

Tiberius shouted out, passionately: "Look at me! You really think I like being a color that separates me from you? You really think I'm proud to have this blood in my veins, this scarlet letter that represents the white world's defeat of my own ancestors? Do you really think I'm beautiful—after so many Africans had to die of broken hearts just so I could be called beautiful? Do you really think this is the natural order when you stand here, on African soil, and look at me?"

"Good speech, na!" hollered a nut-brown girl with a blue-black baby on her hip. "But you move out de way now. I need de Michael Jackson pill for me baby!"

"Doonu!" shouted a university boy. "Open de boxes and start to sell that shit, half-breed. I got classes, man. Hurry!"

But according to Chiamaka, Tiberius had ignored their demands to turn over the loot, pleading with them, "You don't have to look like me to be a human being. You don't have to confirm for the Europeans that you want to be white like them. You don't have to curse your own ancestors, your own African children, and covet their white ones. It's not right for an African to become a nigger. It's not right for an African to become a nigger. It's not right for an African to become a nigger—stay black and live! Stay black and live!"

Chiamaka cried as she related the story. "They started chanting, Eternity. Crowding in on us and chanting, *Kill the Racist! Kill the Racist!* And something in Tiberius just snapped . . . and he welcomed it. He was insane. His eyes clouded with tears and he pleaded against the people's rage. *I love you, my brothers and sisters . . . I love you as you are! You don't need this!* But they stomped and trampled and beat him—for lifting a mirror to their inferiority, for judging them, for loving them, for standing in their way, for being right, for telling the truth, for being racist against whiteness—they killed him."

I couldn't believe it. Killed like I was killed. How could God keep being so cruel?

Supermodel Collapses on Runway
GLOBE ENQUIRER
Add the hot young Eternity Frankenheimer to the list of models rumored to be on drugs. The statuesque West Af-

rican beauty affectionately known as "Charcoal Barbie" recently collapsed on the runway during Giovaldi's show in Milan, and rumor has it she pissed off designers in Paris with the edict that she just couldn't get out of bed—for a whole week. Could it be that she's heartbroken over the recent photos of bad-boy rapper King Sea Horse Twee dancing close with a blond, blue-eyed bombshell in Berlin? Tsk, tsk. We thought we'd seen it all with Naomi Campbell, but now there's a new drama queen in town.

WIMBLEDON 2004

The match seemed to go on forever, but it was the best women's tennis the world had seen in a long time. Russian teenager Maria Sharapova was giving it everything she had, yet in the end was unable to overcome the pure magical athleticism of an aging Venus Williams.

"There are over two hundred American tennis fans here and they all rooted for the Russian—not their fellow American," I pointed out to Sea Horse.

"Oh stop it, your girl Venus won!"

"But the Americans cheered for the Russian girl!"

"Well, aren't you cheering Venus because she looks African like you?" Sea Horse countered. "They cheered Sharapova because they want to see someone who looks like them win. It's human nature, Eternity."

SWEETER AND SWEETER

Tasso Twee, draped in a flowing sky-blue tie-dyed summer dress, matching burka, and huge sunglasses, greeted me at the airfield when I returned home with a huge hug and kiss ("I'm so glad you're back!"). Her eight children welcomed me, tugging and chirping and helping to carry my stuff to the chauffer-driven Mercedes—a comforting arrival. But then, just as we'd gotten my things loaded and I'd climbed into the back of the car, I nearly jumped out of my skin when I noticed a doll—one that resembled me and was the size of a five-year-old child . . . propped up in the backseat.

"It's just a doll of you that I made. Your own likeness," Tasso said sweetly.

"Mama put some of your hair in it," one of the girls said.

"I can't ride in this car, Tasso. I just can't stand dolls. I'm so sorry."

"Eternity, it's a very special doll. We can't leave it here on the airfield. It's your protector. It's taken me months to get the skin color just right, and I took a patch of your clothing and some of your hair. I worked so—"

"Tasso, I just told you, I *hate* dolls!"

She clutched it tightly as she awaited another car to fetch her while the children and I rode away in the Mercedes.

I hadn't meant to yell at her, but everything was about to start going wrong.

From the moment we entered Sea Horse's estate, I was besieged by the worst cravings for something sweet. When you're a supermodel, they give you these all-natural mineral pills to keep you from being hungry—chromium niacin and chromium picolinate—only I was out of my pills, and my bony little hands were shaking.

Dear Eye

In the dreams, it was the stench, the odor of death and sour water,
that pervaded all senses, more so than the dead-eyed fish bodies.

Cut You

"I made this doll to protect you," Tasso said gravely, her burnt-chocolate fingers undoing the lace that covered it like a Christmas present. I wanted to run out of the room, but Tasso's goodwill had come upon me like a net. Her voice was tender as she explained, "While you were gone, I saw you in a casket with your white ma standing over you. Along with ablutions and prayers to Allah, the God Most High, I started carving into the wood with all my willpower."

"You put roots on Sea Horse, Tasso. That's witchcraft."

"No, that's love. And this is love too."

The thing looked just like me.

I told Tasso, "I once had an African mother who made plastic dolls for a living. And she made me practice circumcision on them." A lump grew in my throat, I saw the tiny hands from another life being guided again by Ma Nonni's, cutting the barely developed vaginas of other little girls. I saw blood as deep as chocolate squirting through fingers, braiding the blood-strings. I smelled dead fish, their glass eyes staring at me, I saw hands covered in blood.

And as I fell down on my knees, soulfully weeping at the lives I'd altered in that other life as Orisha, I suddenly realized that Tasso felt threatened by the power of love between me and Sea Horse. She intended to kill me through the doll—which is what traditional jungle wives used to do to people all the time, I'd heard—and I fought to regain my composure.

I said to her simply, "Fuck you, bitch." Then I ratcheted up all the snot and saliva I could muster and spit it straight into Tasso's startled face. "I'm not a believer in what you do! And I don't like dolls!"

Tasso wiped her face. "This doll was to protect you, not cut you."

"Protect me for what, Tasso!?"

"For Sea Horse!" she shouted, incredulously. "Because we're women and he needs us! And for Africa."

KING OF THE WORLD

As the war in Iraq turned into a quagmire of suicide bombings and world protest against the Bush regime, the presidential primary in West Cassavaland went nearly unnoticed. It seemed the long-ignored genocide in Sudan, coupled with the defiant expulsion of whites from Zimbabwe by President Mugabe, took center stage in Western coverage of African news.

Still, the presidential campaign by King Sea Horse Twee became our people's shining hour, galvanizing the nation with hope as he defeated President Yaw Ibrahim in the election.

The people of West Cassavaland were like a great flood rising up an ocean for Sea Horse. By the thousands they crowded past armed soldiers in the streets of Dak-Crete when Sea Horse spoke in front of the state library. His fists pumped in the air while he rapped his promises, brimming with satisfaction as the people chanted, *"Don . . . chiefo . . . baddo!"*

He was the man.

And on the faces of Ibrahim's soldiers was that poker-faced look of despair and regret, because they knew it was on now. No one had ever posed a serious challenge to Ibrahim or the Fatherland Party.

But even with all this good news going on, something dampened the sweetness of victory for Sea Horse. Millicent York, back in London, was dating a white man.

"She sent the goddamned photographs to my own mother!" Sea Horse hollered in a drunken rage. "That bitch! I trusted her with my seeds in her ass! Gave her a son, a mulatto! And now she's fucking a white man!"

"But she's white herself," I reasoned.

"Fuck you!" he yelled. "She's not white."

"Yeah, fuck me, I'll remember that. You Cassavans are always shouting about the devil white man, but you can't wait to get the white woman's cat on your breath!"

How did he think I felt watching him obsess over a white woman? My voice became shallow with sadness as I said, "Maybe her boyfriend after this one will be black, Sea Horse. This man's race doesn't say anything at all about you. You just have an inferiority complex."

"I am superior to any white man! I am an African!"

"Well, the white man is the king of the world," I told him cruelly. "No matter how many white girls you fuck or how high you climb, we Africans are still the ones who were conquered, colonized, and enslaved."

"I'm no nigger—I still have the hair of Africa growing from my scalp. I haven't been conquered. Now get out of my sight before I rip your face off, bitch!"

"Don't come to my room tonight," I muttered with my nose in the air as I brushed past him.

Good.

I had hurt him really bad, and as I went inside to help Tasso chop coconut, I was glad, because he had hurt me too.

Dear Eye

I dreamt that Sea Horse and I were atop the Empire State Building, our naked bodies entwined, the cold November air chilling us to the heart . . . and our kisses so anxious and desperate that neither of us had the courage to open our eyes. The sky had turned as gray as dark smoke from a forest fire—and we looked like mud people up there. The parents of the earth, kissing soil, black as all black put together, for the earth has parents.

And then, of course, we fell.

We fell, but even then we refused to let go or open our eyes.

We fell.

Falling into ribbons of black silk whipping in the wind like the wings of ravens.

On the First Day of Christmas

On the first day of Christmas, my true love gave to me a small mahogany bowl containing the delicate white petals of a beautiful but cursed Central African flower called ngwago.

I was too ignorant to be insulted or outraged as any normal Cassavan girl would have been—being raised by whites, I had no idea of the significance (the nastiness) behind Sea Horse's offering.

He seemed jealous of my relative success, and had complained about what happens "the minute an African woman gets some fame and money." But Chiamaka wold later explain to me that in Central Africa before the 1840s, African villagers from Mbu to Takpe and NookUroo had worn the ngwago flower around the neck and bosom to ward off the wild gorillas that occasionally kidnapped newly married African women and dragged them into the jungle to rape them.

Wu-Chuchu is what the villagers had originally called these particular male nomadic lowland apes who ditched their clans and traveled solo, carefully scoping out villages for wedding parties or young girls, always evading the fire spears, poisoned leaves, and machetes of the men on watch.

Chiamaka explained that once white men discovered the existence of the species and began hunting, studying, and poaching them, the abductions of African brides stopped. Soon the Africans had to deal with a new predator raping their women: *white men*. And so the word Wu-Chuchu had come to mean "white man," and from the 1840s until the early 1960s, the ngwago flower became a reef of shame, tied around the neck and in the hair of any village woman who was raped by a white man.

"So you see," Chiamaka continued, "Sea Horse is still agonizing over Millicent, a white woman, choosing a white man as his replacement. It hurts his pride. He gave you the ngwago to ward off white men he fears will be after you now that you're a movie actress. He's asking you not to submit."

I gasped, suddenly realizing why all manner of African women were laughing hysterically at the recent photographs of me splashed across the world newspapers.

In nearly every one, I had the ngwago flowers tied in my hair.

"Sea Horse wanted people to laugh at you," Chiamaka surmised. "You know how it is when men love you."

ON THE FOURTH DAY OF CHRISTMAS

Back at Sea Horse's compound in the tropical December heat of West Cassavaland, Tasso, Chiamaka, and I delighted in the Dionne Warwick CD I'd brought back from America, the three of us singing, "*If you see me walk'n down the street, and I start to cry . . . each time we meet . . .*"

Garvey, who was away from his grandmother Binata to spend time before Christmas with Tasso's children, came running up to us.

"Mother Eternity, come quick!" the mulatto boy shouted. "It's that doll of you—you've got to see this!"

By the time Garvey, Tasso, Chiamaka, and I made it up to Tasso's bedroom, all of Sea Horse's children were there staring at the doll in wonder.

"Look!" screamed one of the girls, pointing at it. "Somebody beat her up."

I halted in the doorway, taken aback by what looked like fresh knots and bruises swelling across the doll's face.

"No, it's just the wood curling," Chiamaka said hesitantly. But when I looked at Tasso for confirmation, the expression on her face immediately refuted any such logic. She breathed deeply, assessing the doll's busted lip, the eye that was swollen shut—the red gash of a cut on its brow.

"Who removed the lace!?" Tasso demanded.

Garvey swallowed hard, answering, "I heard the wood popping, and I thought I heard a lady crying, so I took the lace off to see what was wrong, Mother Tasso."

"Give me your hands!" Tasso yelled. Garvey placed his yellow hands in her dark brown ones, and she swat him five licks on the palm with a thick schoolhouse ruler. After the last hit, she asked, "You want your father to be proud of you, don't you? You want to impress him?"

"Yes, Mother Tasso," he cowered.

"Then why aren't you consumed by your Koran lessons? Why are you always fidgeting and snooping around this house instead of becoming a son your father can be proud of?"

Of course, this was all about the hair on Garvey's head—the fact that Sea Horse despised his son's lack of an African crown.

"I heard a lady crying," the little boy wailed.

Then Chiamaka hugged Garvey and flashed a look of disapproval. "He's just a child, Tasso!"

At any other time I would have pressed Tasso about Garvey's psychological health, but when I saw pus oozing from the eye of the wooden doll, I remembered that I am a clone, a kind of doll myself.

Kneeling in front of the child, Tasso said, "Allah will bring you the love of your father. Only Allah can change this." She placed a Koran in Garvey's hands and pressed his fingers into the cloth.

"What I want to know," I interrupted, "is who beat the shit out of this doll."

"It's the doll's way of protecting you," Tasso snapped.

"Protecting me how?"

"By showing you the future!"

ON THE EIGHTH DAY OF CHRISTMAS

On the eighth day of Christmas, my true love gave to me a partridge in a pear tree and I laughed joyously at the weird sounds the partridge made as Tasso and Chiamaka rooted the tree next to the pond in the backyard.

I had tasted blood when Sea Horse kissed me after giving me the gift—though there had been nothing in our mouths but the usual sweet saliva. No blood, and yet I had tasted it.

"I love you more than any woman I've ever known," he had pledged with the conviction of a great actor; only without acting. And then he had blithely sniffed the coconut scent of my short-cropped African hair and caressed its minklike softness as though he were warming by a fire, shielding great light, and lamenting eternity all at once.

My son: if Sea Horse Twee is your father, then this is important to me, that you see the ngwago petals blowing in the breeze and our black bodies clinging and humping into one another's like dolphins humping in the ocean's blue clavicle. It is crucial that you see the grace of his hands—because Sea Horse's hands were beautiful and moved not like boxing gloves, but like butterflies—the hands that would soon kill me; murder me; take my life; mangle me. These were the hands that caressed and loved my flesh that day as though my neck were God's finest fabric, they were the hands that held still my mouth and chin so as to plant his kiss of forever. That sweetest of true love kisses that rang in my head and mouth, my throat and bosom, with every thrust of this passionate man's penis, until all we could do was lay still and hold hands, our dark eyes staring at the ceiling as the ancient Dionne Warwick ballad I told you about coated us in robes of light.

PROOF

I hardly ever thought about my mother anymore—so it startled me when I was suddenly consumed by a desire to kill her.

One moment I was perfectly fine, and then the next— Tasso and I spotted a clone of myself in afternoon traffic; an exact replica of me and Orisha.

Perhaps a year younger, perhaps a year older, I don't know, but it was *me*, a prostitute wearing a hole-ridden cotton sundress, a waiflike sparrow darting cautiously and barefoot along the rubber plants at Mars Bay. The sight of this clone literally paralyzed my imagination and my eyes drowned in horror—all I could see was Stevedore and Juliet, the two of them naked in the laboratory, smoking marijuana, snacking on deep-fried breaded pineapple, and duplicating human genes in culture cups; making up people like it was nothing at all. For here was another Eternity, her face withered by the AIDS virus and her head Q-tipped by a shock of raggedy hair—but still it was me, unmistakably.

And as I wept, wondering dreadfully why my parents had kept me but apparently thrown other clones of my DNA out into the wilderness to fend for themselves, I promised God that I would return to Africa Farms and murder my mother.

Sea Horse stood on a podium that New Year's Eve afternoon, the banner and flag of the United Nationalist Motherland Party backing him up as we were surrounded by thousands of Cassavans along the wide clay ruins of Ajowa's ancient city of Mars, the people chanting when he swung his fist in the air and promised them that soon the Twee-Sankofa Madal, the paradise, would be restored.

To Africans, these are impossible dreams, things to be truly thrilled about. And yet there was only a thud in our stomachs, a slow turtle's silence in our eyes—and in the car on the way back to the compound, we held hands so tight it hurt.

Upon arriving home, Tasso's children ran barefoot to the car when we pulled up.

The chauffer stopped the Mercedes and Sea Horse rolled down his window so they could stick their dusty nappy heads through. "She's gone!" one of them yelled. "Oni says she saw her walk into the woods."

"Saw who?"

"The doll, Mama. The doll you made of Eternity. She got up and left the house! She's gone, Mama—*gone*!"

"Where's Garvey?" Tasso asked.

"Studying his Koran. He would have come down and searched in the woods with the rest of us, but he didn't want you to be mad at him, Mama."

FLYING BACKWARD

Last night I drowned in the most horrible dreams. I saw clones, replicas of myself, marching up the road single file toward Mother's AIDS clinic. They were being led by Orisha's mother, Ma Nonni, all of them carrying dolls that were dripping from the vaginal area where they'd been cut. Dr. Juliet was watching from the clinic porch. But when the clones reached her, Ma Nonni was really Stevedore, and the clones were of my daughter Hope, not me. This is what she would look like as a young woman. In greeting, Dr. Juliet handed each clone a chilled glass of Wife of Tarzan poison.

DEAR EYE

I saw a soul song with my eyes. Right before I died, I saw a soul song. Rhythm and adrenaline and fingers popping. The lyric as it was living and not yet composed. I saw a shade of blue more dreary than the "off-key" in true love. I saw the wail caught in his throat, moaning notes of blood. I saw a soul song.

NEW YEAR'S DAY, 2005

I hate this day.

Sea Horse had men tailing me for protection, but I didn't know it. And, of course, the last person I expected to see at my mother's compound was James Lord, but there he was.

He and Dr. Juliet and two of her colleagues, Rolf Switzer and Edwinna Kelp, were clustered together outside the clinic eating watermelon, their white flesh transformed by the noonday heat into a strawberry ice-cream complexion, their eyes beholding my approach with surprise.

I had come to kill my mother, to trick her into drinking a glass of Wife of Tarzan. But the moment I caught her gaze—her aged face marked with such loneliness—all my anger began to dissipate, to splinter with confusion.

As I reached over to embrace her, I hadn't known that James Lord, red-eyed and reefer-smelling, would place his hairy white arm around my waist, falling against the small of my back, before kissing my cheek. "Good to see you, Eternity. You're looking beautiful."

It was so innocent. But Sea Horse's men only saw me being touched by *the white man*.

I hate this day, because it can never be in the past.

Turning to Dr. Juliet, my rage got the best of me and I demanded, "How many did you make?"

Only she knew what I meant, none of the others, and of all the marblelike eyes in their European heads, hers became the coldest, the most blank.

"I saw Orisha," I hissed at her. "A *different* one."

"Darling, we can talk about this later."

"No, Mother, let your guests entertain themselves and we can talk about it now. And what have you done to Hope?"

"Hope is dead and resting and you know I respect that."

I broke down: "I saw myself prostituting—it was me!"

Dr. Juliet kept her calm. She didn't deny it this time. Like a front-office receptionist, she said, "Stevedore's dead, Eternity. He's not here to answer your questions."

Dear son: when your grandmother said those words to my face—to *Orisha's* face—I slapped the shit out of her.

The smack was a certified incident of the taste being knocked out of someone's mouth; Dr. Juliet forgot her own name as her skin was marked in red by my palm and finger imprint.

And I would learn a lot later that when Sea Horse's bodyguards saw the slap from a far-off hiding place, their imaginations had assumed ridiculous things: for instance, that I'd come unannounced and found my "white devil cheating partner" James Lord shacking up with my mother. And by the way he grabbed me and pulled me away from the others, who wouldn't have thought the same foolishness?

It *looked* that way.

A JEALOUS GOD

It's a terrible way to die—to be beaten to death with a person's bare hands, but as you know, it wasn't the first time for me. People had put me out of the world before, a whole mob of them. But this time was much worse, because it was the person who I now loved more than anything on this earth.

His bodyguards gave their inaccurate report, and he met me half a mile before I arrived at the compound. He yanked me from my car, his fists, transformed into stone Dobermans, crushing and pulverizing my face; breaking the bones so that my screams were guttural, gurgling full of blood, and my eyes fell out of their sockets and my brain drew up into a frozen rubbery numbness, ballooning out of my head as he moaned, "White man's whore!"

And yet, because I was outside my body and saw what I call the "soul song" when it happened, I can tell you that there was no hate in his punches. Every single hit was imbued with the most pitiful possessiveness, the naked anguish of need. Fueled by rage and jealousy, of course, but at the same time love.

Love.

Love.

Dear Eye: I know you are shut.

Sea Horse killed me.

Dear Eye: I know you are shut.

Sea Horse killed me!

And because of him, I stopped loving men. Not some men, but *all men*. There was no hate or dislike—just indifference. And I would never be able to love or hate them again.

I was not afraid or the least bit sad. Heaven is peace, my son. The genesis of vision itself. Darkness—black as all black put together, the harmony of goodness in the good, clean dark.

SON

*Once you open a book,
it can never be closed*

To die is to awaken.

A silvery tide crashed against the black-sanded shoreline, and though I felt weak and tired, nothing could overcome me. I was all-powerful and safe, and I felt not only as though I'd been suddenly freed up from the most exhausting dream, I also felt Sea Horse's love, fighting to follow me.

A tar-black boy, barely twelve with stick arms and knot-boned knees, lifted me and carried me through the jungle. I asked him, "What is this place?"

He said, "Reality."

"Do you hear an old scratched-up Dionne Warwick recording?" I asked.

"Of course I do," the boy replied. "This is heaven. Mother plays those all the time."

The boy walked me to the end of a pungent wisteria forest and stopped just at the edge of a cliff that dropped at least fifty miles into the earth.

I jolted my body toward the little boy's chest, alarmed at seeing the deep drop-off to the faraway canyon below us, and because I was afraid, I did not hear the humming of the woman waiting in the jungle mist on the other side of the valley.

"I am Jesus Christ," the boy told me as he gently placed me in standing position on the ground next to him. "You have heard of me, but have not believed in me—I need you to believe that I would never harm you. Everything I've ever done . . ."

Sparrows black and shiny as molten tar gathered around our feet, and the boy was taller, suddenly, and then moments later taller still—until he was a fully grown man standing next to me. His charcoal skin glistened like oiled vanilla stalks and his black onyx eyes riveted me to outer space. It was Sea Horse's face that I saw in his, and I began to weep with longing. I felt the most intense love, I felt cherished and truly free now.

". . . is so that you would reach this moment of flight."

He pushed me!

Over the cliff Jesus pushed me, and then I was in a free fall. I kicked and screamed and flung my arms in a desperate horrid plunge—but then . . . I was the one.

I was flying. Coasting my body into an upward suspension, controlling and arching my muscles as though I were a trained gymnast. Escorted by a cape of sparrows, their glass eyes and crowing beaks directing me to the other side—and when we got there, the naked charcoal man calling himself Jesus Christ appraised me with a smile, his hands on his hips, the thickest, most pendulous penis hanging betwixt his mighty legs, and his boyish stare imbuing me with a father's approval.

I leaned forward as though standing upright on air, no waving of the arms, just sheer willpower, and then I landed on the cliff beside Jesus in a sort of floating bounce. I didn't want to stop! I loved flying, and he laughed, telling me, "Go ahead . . . fly to your heart's content."

And I did. I flew everywhere, nervously urinating in midair and doing twirls and psych-outs of the birds while shadow-flying against the surface of crystal waters and even into the warmth of an orange sun that invited me to touch it, only to discover that it was cake—the sun orange and spongy, delicious as daybreak. I came through clouds that coated my lips, tasting like cream and sugar, and floated serenely over the jungle night, and then, finally . . . my feet touched earth.

A woman called to me, "I am here, Orisha . . ."

The name gave me goose bumps, but then, peering into the clearing, my eyes searching for the woman, I instead saw Stevedore, my dead father. He was tall and pale as ever, his blue eyes lit by the glowing twin moons that hung over the jungle. Standing next to him was the Christ bearing Sea Horse's face. From Stevedore's freckled white throat came the voice of an African woman, admonishing me, "Fear not . . . mother of Christ; wife of Christ; blood of Christ . . . Love is the resurrection, immortal, timeless—the best place."

All-consuming and breathless, I felt the tongue of Jesus Christ enter my vagina and my throat at the same time. I felt the burning reach of my nipples; the sheer perfect nothingness of everything. I was the best place, and I was filled with his penis. I was resurrected.

The Heart
(Will Kill You)

CHAPTER ONE

A tiny lizard hangs from the cracked white ceiling, which is lit by a single yellow lightbulb. Three days after waking from her coma, Eternity's retinas follow the lizard on its trek across the plastered tundra, the bulb's glow burning across the supermodel's mind so that while submerged in anesthesia, it's all she sees.

"She won't have brain damage, right?"

"The coma was only nineteen hours."

Though the tips of Eternity's toes tingle beneath their stiffness, it's in her buttocks, her neck, ears, and heart that the crashing sound of the sea bounces and reverberates like oxygen igniting blood cells. She's an earthling again.

Nineteen hours.

The surgeon's powerful black hands grip her face like a steering wheel, bending bone and suctioning blood until the reconstruction of her countenance becomes a symphonic process at odds with the gut-bucket soul song that in another life accompanied the boxerlike fists as they'd beaten and smashed her heart away. At times, under heavy sedation, Eternity thinks she hears a drum-roll or a skateboard, but no—it's Sea Horse's heartbeat.

"Now and forever," he calls. This man has the face of Jesus Christ, and yet he is the one who killed her. His eyes lick and caress her with a childish hopefulness, his heartbeat thumping like a prayer beneath her consciousness, but still, the thing about beat-up women and the men who beat the shit out of them is that only they can interpret the sounds; and just as one can never set eyes on the same river twice, a reconfigured face has new expressions too.

"Young lady, do you recall what your name is?"

"Eternity?"

"Yes, very good. What is your tribe?"

"Ajowan?"

"Yes. What did the nurses feed you this morning?"

"Stock fish and sweet milk?"

"Yes."

"I don't feel she's back," whines the one who looks like Jesus Christ but killed her.

After a little more than a week, as the bandages come off and the swelling subsides (she is too dark to show bruising), Sea Horse grows more and more despondent and the men argue.

"She looks just like her magazine covers from before," the plastic surgeon insists, but tears fill the eyes of Sea Horse Twee.

"No, she was a mermaid when I found her. That's not her face. It's not the same!"

"Look, I've done everything possible—"

"But something's different!"

"Well, it wasn't me who bashed her face in!"

"It wasn't me either!" Sea Horse lies.

"The patient vanished for more than half a day—nobody comes back from that the same."

"But I paid a fortune to fix her face!"

"She looks beautiful. I don't know what you expect."

"It's my love . . . but it's not her!" Sea Horse breaks into sobs like a child.

"My dear God, Brother Twee, keep your wits about you . . ."

Sea Horse falls to his knees, proclaiming, "I killed her! It's my love, but it's not her—I killed her!"

CHAPTER TWO

An appeaser is one who feeds a crocodile, hoping it will eat him last, goes the popular saying in West Cassavaland. Now, like light breaking through a doorway, Tasso Twee, with her hands soaking wet from having just bathed the wooden doll she'd made to protect Eternity, stood at the top of the stairs and watched as the foyer of her home upended like a landmine. Eternity's body was draped by sheets of white-paper hospital gowns, her feet dangling as Sea Horse carried her over the threshold. "Eternity's home!" the children cheered. But between Tasso and Sea Horse, there was no smiling. The doll was all they contemplated. In fact, down the hall in Tasso's bathroom, the doll sat in a tub of bluish bathwater, its wooden lips creasing from absorption as the wetness on Tasso's hands dried by air.

"The nurse here yet?" Sea Horse asked.

Tasso nodded.

"Biapa nuli tafa" (Be a good wife), Sea Horse commanded.

"I'll prepare your bedroom," Tasso answered obediently, floating away with her head held as high as she could possibly hold it.

IT HAS TO BE DONE

Almost everyone at the compound noticed a change in Sea Horse—a paradigm shift, in fact—in both his mental and emotional range since the beating, temporary death, coma, and hospitalization of Eternity Frankenheimer. But as sensitive and soft-footed as he'd suddenly become, Tasso also knew that her husband's time for bringing the message of the Twee-Sankofa Madal paradise was quite short.

God Sakhr (Satan) had appeared to Tasso during a nap, barefoot in the field of all the harvests she'd ever had with Sea Horse. In the fog of that same field she had seen Allah, the Holy Father, but with His back to them, as God will do when He leaves animals to the earth. Although Tasso herself was a powerful witch possessing the will of Sanna (the virtue of all the dead wives of her tribe) and had only taken on the title of Muslim at her husband's behest, there was nothing she could do to stop the devil.

People by the thousands—for instance, the Pogo Metis Signare and the corporate politicians of Europe and America who stood to lose power with Sea Horse as president—had put the will of their hatred into the universe with great intensity. Just as a powerful hostility had become telepathic enough to mow down Malcolm X, the American Kennedys, and Lumumba, the same thoughts and feelings were now aimed at smiting Tasso's husband.

Sea Horse Twee was going to die, and all she had hoped was that there would be a final son born through Eternity's fresh young womb. And for that reason, she moved everything in the universe to protect whatever

seed might arise from God's closing of one door and opening of another. Nothing that Tasso did was about herself.

Carefully, she fluffed the pillows and fitted the sheets
on her marriage bed—a bed that had abided so many
more women than just herself.

It hurt all through her—but like the African clans-
women who had taught her the art of being a wife, Tasso
set aside her own wants in order to serve that which she
thought was natural order for the village, the people. Sea
Horse, a great and important leader, was going to die—
but perhaps through her efforts neither his vision nor
his message for West Cassavaland would die with him.

"Even in death, a son who is a gift to his people must
never perish," Tasso muttered as Sea Horse entered the
room carrying Eternity to the bed.

It has to be done, Tasso thought, nervously. *Wait till he
leaves the room . . . then do it.*

"Tasso, can you get her some fresh water?"

"It's there already, by the bed."

"You think of everything," he said, pleased.

Like a hawk, Tasso studied the way Eternity's dull,
dark eyes bore into Sea Horse's face, the way her body
stiffened with fear; while in Eternity's mind, she was
wondering how God could be so cruel as to put the same
face on Jesus Christ and Sea Horse Twee.

"Pace yourself," Tasso whispered, spying the dev-
astation in Sea Horse's misty eyes. "The heart will kill
you."

She pulled him back from the bed and forced a glass
of tamarind juice into his hands. Though he couldn't
dare take his eyes off Eternity, at least he drank the
juice, thought Tasso.

Wearily, she persuaded Sea Horse to review the white notebooks that covered his bureau, each one open to pages where Tasso had been diligently composing his upcoming political speeches.

Africa has been cloned! he read on one page.

Sea Horse blinked to comprehend, but he liked the concept, finding it powerful and evocative of many rebellious plans simmering in his mind.

Yes, thought Sea Horse, *fuck the G8 with their welfare checks and slave loans,* breaking into a mild sweat. He planned to cut off from the G8, the World Bank, the International Monetary Fund.

"Come back to us, Africa," he muttered.

JESUS AND MARY

Later that night, the wooden doll stood fully dressed in the mansion's hallway as if preparing for a night out.

"There's a light missing from her eyes now," Tasso told Sea Horse. "If I hadn't carved that doll to protect her from the blows, her spirit would be separated from the flesh and bones as well."

Sea Horse, who was high and steadily smoking a pile of the best marijuana in DakCrete, glanced at the doll standing in the hallway before responding, "You little African witch—you saw what I did to her, didn't you? You saw me beat her to death, didn't you?"

Tasso nodded.

"What were you doing there?"

"I went to bathe in the shallow pond with the silver minnows, but when I peered at the bottom, the ancestors showed me everything."

"Then why have you said nothing?"

"Because I knew I could save her for you," Tasso replied. "I will stand for you."

"But I killed her. She has a body now, but I smothered her spirit."

"You can bring it back," Tasso said. "God has promised that your erection is our resurrection, enshalla—woman is man's church. That is how you will bring her back to us."

"She won't even look me in the eye or talk to me, let alone—"

"If it be done with love, the penetration—the African way, sweet King, your purest, purest love—it will bring her back. Man's erection is the resurrection."

Tasso then retrieved the large doll and showed Sea Horse the new carving she'd made, a slit and a hole in its crotch.

"I used a little blood from my own vagina and a little fish oil to humanize the bark," she explained.

Sea Horse touched his fingertips to the opening of the doll's wooden vagina, then observed, "There's a human part to it now."

"The force of life is everywhere," Tasso replied. "Woman is man's church, Sea Horse. Man's erection is our resurrection. You were made to love her, to heal her."

Just then, Garvey stormed into the room. "Father, come quickly! The nurse told me to tell you that Eternity's run away—"

CHAPTER THREE

Eternity Frankenheimer didn't want to model or be around people that year. She rented a lavish apartment in DakCrete and floated about its rooms consumed by a deadbolt silence. She surfed idly online, typing *LOL* in place of actually laughing. This was the new world order and she was sedated to it.

But one day, when she was sitting with the old Oluchi women at the river near her mother's clinic, they took pity on her and inadvertently set in motion the rebirth of her spirit. They showed her a photograph of her dead daughter, Hope, amazingly back alive and sporting a sagging diaper and a pacifier as she grinned, waving from Dr. Juliet's arms in the marijuana field behind the clinic.

It shocked Eternity into a different type of sedation. Back at her apartment, she couldn't stop staring at the photo.

Soon, reading a *New York Times* article about cloned pigs, Eternity was absolutely floored by the revelation that Harvard Medical School, the University of Missouri, and the University of Pittsburgh Medical Center were all experimenting with the process of cloning animal parts to modify food sources. Scientists explained how they had taken enzymes from microorganisms like plankton and algae and introduced them into the body structures of mice, pigs, and rabbits.

The words reminded Eternity of dinner table conversations from her childhood at Africa Farms AIDS Clinic; now the language had spread to the rest of the world.

Yet Eternity remained despondent with the knowledge that Juliet had cloned her daughter. Eventually, she'd gotten in touch with the maid Fergie and paid her to keep tabs and report back to her.

"There's something I haven't told you, Eternity," Fergie admitted over the phone one evening.

"What is it, Fergie?"

"I don't want you to take this too hard, but there's not just one baby."

"What!"

"There are two."

"That sick bitch!" Eternity hissed. "This is exactly what they did to me—they made multiple Orishas."

Fergie corrected her: "No, there are two babies, Eternity, but they are not both from your daughter Hope. The other infant is a boy with red hair, freckles . . ."

OhmyGod!

Father.

In slow-motion, Eternity saw her father, Stevedore, gulping down the toxic Wife of Tarzan that had killed him.

She's cloned Father.

CIGARETTE

Sex calmed her.

James Lord had been begging to see her, so she invited him to spend a few days at her apartment in DakCrete.

Her tongue dueled against his tongue; his firm hairy chest pressed down against her feverish charcoal breasts, his mouth and his crotch consuming both openings like a blanket of comfort while his white buttocks bounced joyfully between her long, licorice-black legs; and in a way that reminded her of her father, James's hard, passionate penetration thrilled her with the masculinity that she loved, craved, and was always soothed by.

This, along with sleep and a good meal, she thought, was the best part of life. James Lord banged her with a final gallop—his face twisting into a moaning growl as he ejaculated deep within her.

The next morning in bed Eternity admitted, "I'm not interested in being in love."

"We've just been reunited, and before I can order up roses you're traipsing back to Sea Horse . . . Eternity, I need you to be up front—how do you feel about us?"

"How do you feel about your goddamned cryptids, James? You're the one dredging some lake in the Congo looking for a mythical water monster that you believe the capturing and documenting of will somehow make you into a real man! You white men are all alike—always searching the fucking universe for something to unearth that's none of your business! What is this God complex that white men have?"

James Lord laughed. "You're the only mythical monster I'm interested in proving my manhood to, Eternity. And don't think I don't know about your birth control. You've been skipping it."

Eternity froze. Yes, they had been fucking like bunnies for three days and she had been skipping it.

"You planning on being knocked up?" James smiled.

"I personally wouldn't mind a pregnant supermodel keeping me company on that lake in the Congo."

"Is that the story this year, James?"

"I've offered to marry you before."

Box of Ballots

Word quickly swept across the planet that Sea Horse Twee had won the election in West Cassavaland.

They elected him king!

In stunned silence and staring at the television news coverage, Eternity watched as the handsome rapper-turned-politician shocked the world by shaking his fist before a roaring crowd and shouting, "To hell with globalization! Africa is a clone, nothing but a clone of itself—but, great ancestors, I promise you: no more!"

Nearly a million Cassavans were gathered outside the White House cheering and screaming to his every admonition. Women in labor all over Africa were naming their newborn children Sea Horse—whether they were boys or girls, it didn't matter.

"I bring you respect," Sea Horse said to the mass of black faces.

Dressed in a flowing bone-white dashiki with a Ghanaian Ashetu on his head, with Tasso and his mother Binata standing regally beside him, president-elect Sea Horse Twee ripped up a stack of official-looking papers and shouted, "There will be no more G8 for the kings and queens of West Cassavaland!"

"*You go put die! You go put die!*" screamed the ooh-Luck.

"There will be no more blond wigs on the court bench judges, no more European-tailored suits in the legislature—from now on, every African politician will attend the government of this nation wearing our traditional African clothes, the clothes of our mighty forefathers!"

It was rumored that Sea Horse was now romancing the breathtakingly beautiful chocolate-skinned woman standing off behind Tasso, the Nigerian movie goddess Genevieve Nnaji. Eternity, in a rash of jealousy, sighed and fell back to earth.

Sea Horse ended his address by reciting West Cassavaland's "Poem of Patriotism," words that had been erected by proud African men on the day of the nation's independence: "*For we are the Africans . . . the children of the earth's first garden . . . that perfect, deliberate blackness that can only be described as the genesis of vision itself. Let freedom ring.*"

With the deepest breath, Eternity's spirit was inching its way back. Wet between the legs, she went to him.

GRAPE

"Open your eyes now," President Sea Horse said.

Eternity did as commanded, the curves of her sensuous body quivering with guilt and shame as her lips burned with anticipation for the delectable surprise he would soon feed her.

"Gently touch them with your tongue," he continued.

She knew she had no business being there in the White House—in his bathing chateau while one of the maids rubbed her body down with warm oils. She touched her tongue erotically to several juicy black grapes hanging from Sea Horse's hand, then devoured them.

She explained to him how overwhelming it had felt,

how horrifying and sickening it had been, to come face-to-face with the newly spawned infant versions of her dead child, Hope, and her father, Stevedore.

Dr. Juliet's reefer-mad eyes had held her with a shameless defiance.

Eternity, of course, had lost it upon the sight of little Hope and Stevedore peeking up from a bassinet in the nurses' station hall. They didn't recognize Eternity from Adam. They were so innocent; just babies.

She had burst into tears and run out of the clinic, but Juliet tried to calm her down.

All Eternity could think was, *White people—the lonely white people.*

Lonely, restless, well-meaning, adventuring aimlessly across the earth in search of love.

Here's the Internet—love me. Here's a flu vaccine—love me. Here are scissors to cut things with—love me.

Here are submarines to submerge into another world with—love me. Here is a satellite in space to view football—love me.

Here is my portrait of Jesus Christ—love me.

Here, I'm taking over your country, so we can live together.

Love me.

Here, I brought you back to life.

Love me.

Stay for dinner. Mothers need love too.

Love me.

Eternity Frankenheimer had fallen to pieces, unable to stay angry at her mother but eager to speed away from the clinic.

Love me.

* * *

Violently, he tasted her, his bone-white teeth and his rapturous tongue sucking and mowing into the yoke of Eternity's swanlike neck.

Eternity's long black legs opened to receive his penis as the gob of juicy grapes fell against the floor and his large hands bore down on her bare shoulders like the paws of a jungle panther pinning down fresh antelope pussy.

In deep measures he took it—the tight, sweet charcoal pussy that far and away had become his favorite.

Striving, poking, and lunging until every poetic coo from her softly straining neck was a prayer rising up; grateful and sanctified by the pure, ever-aging call of two lone ancient words: *Love me.*

Eternity broke.

The ohms of her throat cracking like whiplash.

She fell into the realm of blindness . . .

(And on the second floor of the White House, in the bedroom beneath Sea Horse's bathing chateau, Tasso Twee was awakened by the faint smell of smoke and little snaps of bursting flames. Her eyes opened and her body jumped into sitting position as she realized that the doll was catching on fire on its stand. It crackled and popped into a blue-flamed rage while Tasso clapped her hands together and erupted with laughter, screaming and shouting, "I did it, I did it!")

Eternity pressed her hand against his chest—her head back in blindness as the rhythm of his hips and the large penis attached to it shook and be-danced her like gravel in a seabed.

Diving, loving, reaching . . . possessing.

Son . . .
Son . . . my eyes opened!
I felt . . . falling.
I was falling and falling . . .

DEAR EYE (OPEN)

Son!

Oh my son. I was back!

Sea Horse's erection evoked in me . . . a resurrection.
Life.

I could see it again—the soul song from my death.

My spit dragging with his lips as he removed his
mouth from my mouth and caressed the smoothness of
my skin-only head, his eyes peering deep into mines, his
heart calling me back from feelings and images that even
now I can't define.

One moment, he was Sea Horse the mortal. The next,
he wasn't Sea Horse at all—but this figure the world's
men have made up to represent their penis symbol, Jesus Christ.

The scripture unrolling like ribbons against harsh
winds.

His mouth vowing, "I love you, woman—I love you."

TEACHER DON'T TEACH ME NONSENSE

I cringed hearing the words, because after being beaten
to death by a black man's hands twice in two lifetimes—
there was no way in the world I would ever love a man
again.

It just wasn't necessary.

We Who Go with
the Landscape

I love you, my son, your little feet kicking and your tiny hands balling into fists as your dark celestial-eyed stare flickers like blinks of intelligence against the orbit of my own. You, the one who grew inside me for nine months—it's you I love.

"What will you name him?" the giggling nurses at DakCrete City Medical Center asked excitedly after you were born and were placed in my arms. Just as I'd expected, their girlish smiles turned to frowns when I gave them the answer.

They couldn't have understood what the miracle across your chest meant to me—the three nipples that they considered a deformity. In fact, they'd covered one with a bandage and taped a crucifix over it—superstitious bullshit that I immediately ripped away, because I wanted to see it, that third nipple.

My God, the smile on my face as I thought of Tiberius again, and the miracle of it all—the miracle!

Perhaps Jesus Christ was your papa and not Sea Horse or James, I thought. Then I laughed, kissing and kissing your chest with my eyes closed, sweetly blessing you.

I told the nurses, "His name will be Eternity . . . same as mines. Like his mother, he's forever."

"What about the father's name?" the head nurse objected. "A boy, especially first-born, should be named after the father."

"I don't know who the father is."

KASHA! Their mouths fell open in shock as their Christian stares turned to Christian stones.

The wedding ring on my finger is what did it—the fact that I was a married woman. What kind of African woman marries a man while pregnant and then doesn't even know who the father is?

"She thinks she's European," one of them hissed before storming off in disgust.

But, honestly, who needs those women?

All I cared about then, Eternity, was that you were here and healthy and snuggled safe in my arms—your warm, tender little face against my breast, suckling, and already the dang-nap crown of our ancestors breaking through your precious black scalp.

And all I care about now is that as my son and closest, most trusted confidante, you understand why I did what I did following Sea Horse's assassination.

WITH THIS RING

Not just West Cassavaland but all of Africa was afire with elation at the victory of King Sea Horse Twee.

Almost to the seventh month of my pregnancy with you, it was like our very own Camelot.

Sea Horse had opened the White House for what was to be his annual "Picnic with the People." His British record company doled out miles of free hot food as he shut down Spy Control, emptied their torture prisons, and then drafted a ten-year plan for national literacy, making it mandatory that all Cassavan children be taught to read and write if nothing else.

First Lady Tasso Twee became the continent's model

of elegance, style, and old-ways subservience. Images traveled around the world showing her and Sea Horse's row of proud Cassavan-faced children, as well as the one child who stood out from the rest: slick-haired, light-skinned Garvey, whose heartbroken eyes stared out from the magazine covers as though he were some Lebanese neighbor's child and not a Twee.

I should have seen it coming, but I was too happy.

The mullahs in the Arab industrial nations took their cues from the smiley-faced white politicians and corporate heads in the Western world, and had discreetly gotten word to Garvey's teachers that his father was to be killed and that he—such the devoted learner of Islam because it pleased his father—was to be the vessel, the bomb.

Explosives were strapped across innocent little Garvey's torso beneath robes of satin, his face conflicted by honor, duty, and confusion. But still, he'd kept the secret and had taken his place on Sea Horse's lap during a photo op on the White House lawn, and then—BOOM!—the two of them ignited in an orange and black fire, exploding into smithereens.

And that was that.

Allah before father, flesh, and family.

There weren't even bodies left to bury.

In no time, President Yaw Ibrahim the Black was put back in office, Spy Control reopened and rounded up and imprisoned many of Sea Horse's most ardent political deputies, and the Pogo Metis Signares returned to the legislature—every single one of them dressed in expensively cut European suits.

Nothing but silence gripped our nation, because it

seemed that everything we'd ever loved had left us.

As a gesture to the masses, Sea Horse's birth date was declared a national holiday by the returning government and Tasso Twee was given the honorary yet ultimately meaningless title Official Queen of West Cassavaland.

At Sea Horse's funeral, the press corps photographed me, very pregnant, weeping next to the casket, and the image went all around the world, reporters in every nation declaring you his unborn child.

But not James Lord. No, James was certain, beyond a shadow of a doubt, that you are his son. And considering all the times he and I made love, how can I disagree?

Yet staring into the casket that day, I wanted to believe that you are by Sea Horse. I needed to.

The emotional turmoil soon got to me and I was hospitalized for depression.

At the hospital, I realized that it was Sea Horse who had finally made me African—he had connected me and gave me a sense of being whole. Without him in the world, I suddenly felt lost, naked, and frightened.

Not knowing what else to do, I said yes when James Lord came to my bedside and asked me to be his wife.

He immediately sold my apartment in DakCrete and bought a bungalow for us to live in on Sabu-Nu beach while we waited for you to be born.

Cassavans hurled bottles and cans at us when I was wheeled out of the hospital holding my wedding bouquet—"Traitor bitch!" they called. "She married a Caucasoid!" But all I had done was try to rescue my sanity.

I had lived through so much hardship in my lifetimes, and frankly, I was tired of living.

But you kept me alive.

THE WHITE MAN IS NOT THE DEVIL

As a black woman in a white supremacist world, I can't honestly claim that I've suffered any more prejudice and mistreatment from white men than I have from my own black men. Both groups seem to live by the white man's standard, so they both hate, degrade, exploit, and humiliate black women, fail to even acknowledge our presence. Yet when it comes to race loyalty, I always took the side of the black man—not because he was morally superior to the white man, but because he's the one I give birth to, the one my womb produces.

In Africa we talk a lot about the Great White Devil, the innate evilness of the white race, but the real truth, Eternity, is that the white man and the black man are probably the same man—the world is just ruled and trampled upon by the one who got to the gun first. And unfortunately, the one with the spear has been struggling at the foot of the one who got to the gun first ever since—but they're the same man, capable of the same genius, the same goodwill, and the same inhumanity.

Neither is superior to the other.

Two days before you were born, Sea Horse's lawyers showed up to tell me about the island he'd left me in his will.

"Love Bird Island," they informed me, "is four hundred miles off the coast where West Cassavaland meets Senegal, Mrs. Lord. International waters, so there's no jurisdiction by any sovereign states. You can do whatever you want out there."

218)(THE SEXY PART OF THE BIBLE

"An island—Sea Horse left me an island?"

"Two hundred and seventy-four acres of white beaches, exotic plants, towering palm trees, and a two-story cottage mansion."

"You could start your own country," another lawyer joked.

THE RIVER PASSED, AND GOD FORGOTTEN

Dreams that you thought were impossible and had long ago given up on, my son, you'll find that they tide back into your consciousness, and no matter what you've been raised to believe or how you try to fit other people's expectations of what you're supposed to be, some of the dreams inside you are much bigger than just you—in fact, you'll find that there was a you before you were you.

I couldn't shake it, Eternity. My people's dream of the Twee-Sankofa Madal—their dream of paradise.

The London *Guardian* was the first to break the story: *Bitter Supermodel-Actress Files Petition to Establish Her Own Nation*.

People thought I was crazy.

In America, there was a headline plastered above my face: *No Bitch Is an Island!*

"Why do you want a divorce?" James demanded.

"Because I don't want just one man anymore," I told him, honestly.

"How many men do you want?"

"I don't know, James. I adore you and I don't think I'll ever stop adoring you, but I've finally realized that

I could be a lot happier if I had my space here on the island and kept multiple boyfriends around the world."

"A bloody cum-catcher!" he cursed. "You'd rather be a whore than a respectable married lady?"

I nodded.

He stared at me as though I were diseased.

"What's happened to you? You're not the same woman. What about my love for you? I love you!"

"I don't love men anymore, James. The whole religion of male rule . . . I've died and gone to heaven and come back and now I don't love men anymore. I want them . . . when I want them. Just like you are your own man, I want to be my own woman. I want to enjoy a variety of different men—when I feel like being bothered."

LONER

Finally, to the world's shock—I did it!

Due to the fact that my island lay in international waters and was under a non–property tax–paying jurisdiction that constituted *terra nullius*, sovereign state laws and federal courts in both West Cassavaland and Senegal officially recognized me as a micronation and allowed me to rename my island what my Ajowan ancestors had originally called West Cassavaland—*Ajowaland*.

I started my own country; founded my own nation.

I named my capital city New DakCrete and sent immigration offers to half a dozen young, hard-working African dock boys who began building a village of thatch-roofed dome houses for themselves and their girlfriends to live in. I would call my citizens "Eternalists."

I was the nation of Ajowaland's standard of beauty!

Charcoal me! A flag that looked like the starry blackness of outer space waved from a pole in front of my mansion and was duly registered as the official flag of Ajowaland.

I couldn't think of a national motto right away, but my country's national anthem was Sea Horse Twee's final hit single, "We Who Go with the Landscape."

> *If there is memory, then there is a mother*
> *Blood of the ancestors . . . their blood uncolonized*
> *Black as all black put together*
> *We who are left . . . we who go with the landscape*

A black American woman in Chicago wrote me an e-mail:

> *Girl, my name is Ronette Marie Sheridan. I'm a bookkeeper at Chicago City Hall. I read in the newspaper you done had the nerve to start your own damn country. Can I come be a citizen? I'm black, thirty-four, two children—a boy and a girl. I heard your requirement for full citizenship is nappy hair and brown-to-black skin. Well, I'll tell you this, Miss Charcoal Barbie—we may be yellow, but we got some nappy-ass hair, girl.*

Then two brothers from Kenya wanted to immigrate— and Chiamaka and her new husband came.

My favorite photographer, Casper, visited with his boyfriend, Israeli gymnast Zorn Lieber.

Rector Sniff from M magazine arrived with his cameras and asked me, pointedly, "I've heard of recluses, Eternity, but do tell—what made you so bitter against the rest of humanity? What made you a separatist?"

HOLLYWOOD

Some months later, I went to visit that flat, never-ending, lights-on-a-pizza city known as Los Angeles to make the television miniseries *Kamit-Ama, African Goddess*, but they did it to me all over again.

The producers, studio executives, finance officers, and all-around race-deniers got down to business and decided that I was too black to play a black woman.

In fact, the Americans decided that every woman in West Cassavaland was too black and nappy, too Negroid-faced, to represent what we actually look like, what our actual beauty looks like.

They instead cast an African mulatto and surrounded her with male actors who looked like Djimon Hounsou, Don Cheadle, and Taye Diggs—you know how they do in Hollywood.

Killing and killing with images that gradually erase us.

I don't care what the black Americans and British try to tell you when you grow up, my son—a wood log may float atop a river a hundred years, but it will never be a crocodile.

Look what they did to Kamit-Ama!

I wanted to kill everybody in America for such hypocrisy and blindness, but then I realized: it's not my country.

It's not my country.

I will never have representation from those racists and their fifty-six shades of plantation-raised Afro-zombies. It's impossible, because through my black womb, little black boys like you cannot be erased from their land-scape. So, you see, it's me who they have to erase first.

After losing the miniseries, my agent sent me to lunches with several black American film directors, all men—but fishing for parts from them turned out even worse.

Whereas swashbuckling white men had told me all my life that I was beautiful, I was suddenly surrounded by hip young black American men who seemed embar-rassed by my bald head, shocked that my color was real (not computer generated), and whose standoffish glances inferred that I was not just ugly, but no part of them whatsoever. Though their black American lips, noses, and foreheads were unmistakably of a West Af-rican mother-seed, some would say things like, "They got some fine bitches in Ethiopia"—and because of that rejection, it occurred to me that perhaps men like Steve-dore and James weren't so taken by my beauty as they were by me being an oddity, a kind of rare alien artifact. A cryptid.

I tell you now: no pure African woman should ever set up house in the United States or Great Britain.

It's my image that they ban from the screen, so that you lose the memory of your real mother's face, my beauty in its full, perfect darkness. Then, through their sanctioned Pogo Metis Signare girl, they begin to erase you as well. And I can't tolerate that.

I love to laugh about how Hollywood and the black Americans treat me now, because this island is my re-venge, the proof that I will never be erased.

KOLA BOOF)(223

INDIGENOUS

I love you, my son.

I no longer fear dolls.

I guess I can let you go now.

You are getting bigger and more independent by the day, Eternity—your manish black legs jetting across the white beaches as you leap and fly like a spear into the clear surf, engaging my sense of adventure and reminding me of the freedom-loving Sea Horse and his enthusiastic way of making love to the ocean. He swam with his hips as you do—it's the way black men dance, you know, with their hips.

You're growing so fast.

I miss him.

I guess I can let you go now . . .

On warm sea-soothing evenings when the religion of man's penis flutters beneath my smirking contemplation, I taste sweet clarity knowing that my atheist woman-reflecting charcoal vagina has brought yet another black man into the world, and that this reproduction is indeed Africa in its purest most realistic state; the earth's first religion being my black pussy.

Queen Tasso and her children come to visit us and I shake my head, wondering how I survived all that I have been through, because I'm not even thirty years old (this time); and yet, sitting on the porch serving peppercorn chicken wings and iced tea, my bony hands picking up a comb with which to scratch Tasso's scalp, laughing and talking, braiding her soft, springy jungle of nappy hair—it's as though I'm the living and the dead all in one, and I know enough to say, "Fear not."

It's because of you I've decided . . . I do have a soul.

Don't be afraid, I let you go.

Don't be afraid.

Swim, son; your heart rises and falls with the knowledge that nothing truly African can ever escape Africa. Other bitches try to wear my face. The world over; other bitches try to wear my face. But here, black as all black put together—the genesis of vision itself—I am Eternity's mother. I am the one who said, *Beauty is when you look like your own people.* "Ife kwulu ife akwudebe ya" (If one thing stands, another thing stands by it). This is we, the Eternity . . . accept no imitations.